OF TAILS & MISTLETOE

NATALINA REIS

HOT TREE PUBLISHING

Of Tails and Mistletoe

OF MAGIC AND SCALES 3.5

NATALINA REIS

HOT TREE PUBLISHING

Also by Natalina Reis

M/M Stand-alone Romances

Infinite Blue

Lavender Fields

Sleeping Love

Of Magic & Scales Series

Of Magic and Scales

Of Scales and Fire

Of Fire and Bone

Of Tails & Mistletoe

M/F Stand-alone Romances

Loved You Always

Blind Magic

Fictional-ish

Her Real Man

The Jewel Chronicles

Desert Jewel

Rebel Jewel

Snow Jewel

Of Tails and Mistletoe © 2021 by Natalina Reis

Of Tails and Mistletoe is a work of fiction. All names, characters, events and places found therein are either from the author's imagination or used fictitiously. Any similarity to persons alive or dead, actual events, locations, or organizations is entirely coincidental and not intended by the author.

For information, contact the publisher, Hot Tree Publishing.

www.hottreepublishing.com

Editing: Hot Tree Editing

Cover Designer: BookSmith Design

Ebook ISBN: 978-1-922359-92-6

Paperback ISBN: 978-1-922679-08-6

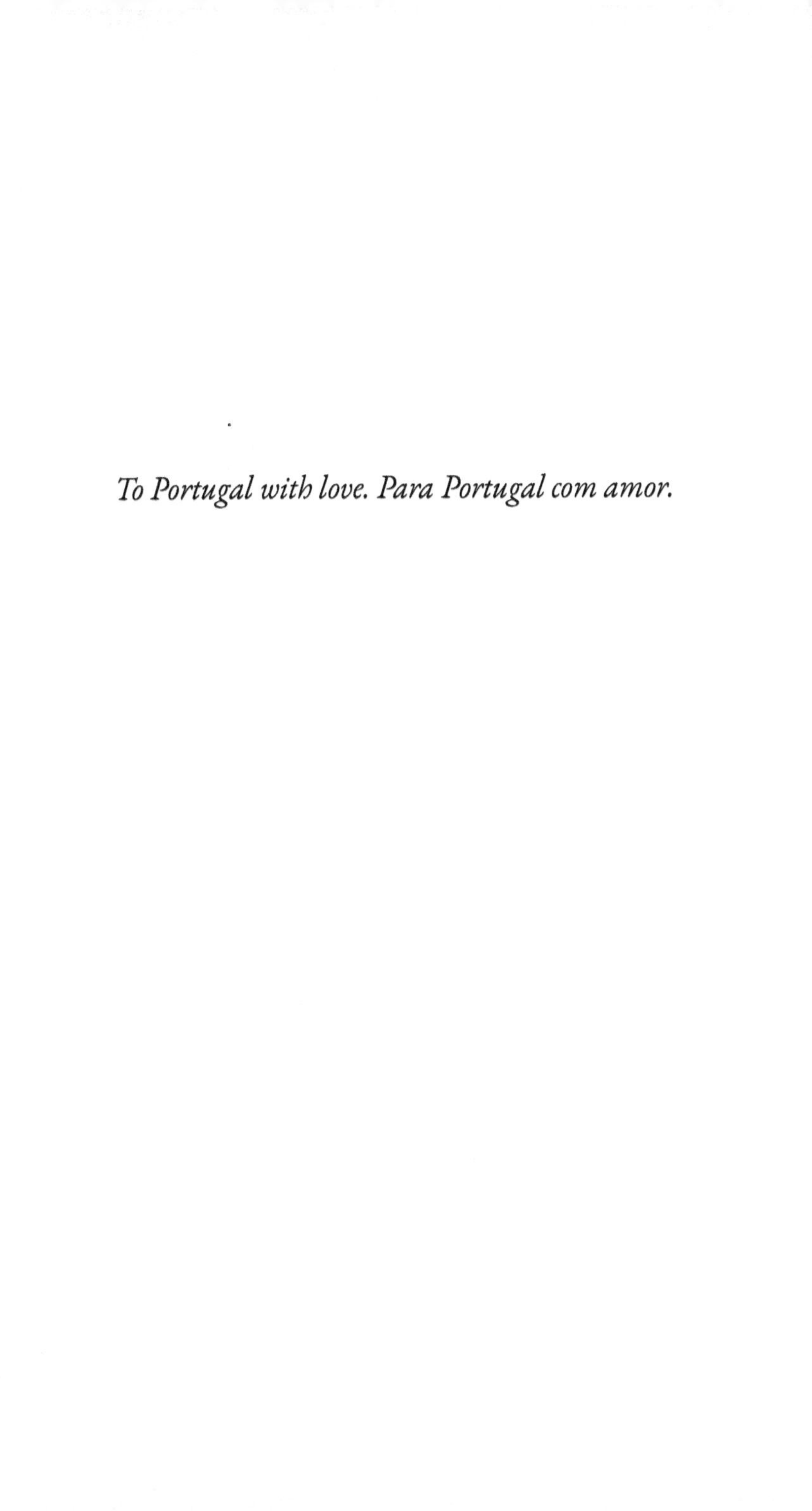

To Portugal with love. Para Portugal com amor.

CHAPTER 1

O Come Ye, All Ye Magicals

If I heard "Jingle Bells" one more time that morning, I was going to summon my fireballs—no dirty pun intended—and destroy the mall's PA system. My soul mate and all-around hot guy, Naël, was annoyingly undisturbed by the incessant hammering of peppy Christmas music as he wandered from store to store, his collection of giant shopping bags multiplying by the minute. I gingerly carried my one and only bag, a tiny red number where a simple piece of jewelry hid—my Christmas gift for Cristina.

My merman scanned me with suspicion in his big brown eyes. "Is that all you are going to buy?" he asked, pointing at the miniature bag in my hand. "No more Christmas gifts? What about something for the baby?"

I shrugged. "I'm ordering gift cards online for everybody else and the baby isn't due for months," I declared, sniffing the air to locate the nearest coffee stall. "You are marrying *me*. Why would you need another gift?"

Naël barked a laugh and drew me in for a hug. "True, sweetheart. Who needs gifts when I have you in my bed every night?"

We made a stop at the bookstore on the way out, and by the time we got home, I was lugging a large canvas bag full of books. Naël kept throwing dubious glances at me and smirking. I would not apologize for being a bookworm.

Vee greeted us at the door, flushed and wearing the most god-awful mermaid-inspired outfit. We had hoped that her foray into the tweens would have sharpened her sense of style, but apparently, we had both been very off. If anything, her obsession with everything mermaid and unicorn had risen to the level of madness. Her room was currently an explosion of rainbows and pastels that caused tooth decay to any who ventured in.

"Guess who's here?" she asked, throwing herself at her brother's neck. Naël blew a few of her almost-white curls off his face. "Oisin is here," she blurted out a second later. Which meant the witch, Taz, wouldn't be far. Those two had something going on or my name wasn't Aiden.

"You seem a bit too excited about Oisin," Fouchard said, disentangling himself from his sister's arms. "Did he buy you a unicorn or something?" He was a god after all; maybe he could indeed get her a unicorn.

Vee's amber face darkened. "Wait! Are you blushing?" *Did Vee have a crush on the Celtic god?* "Do you have the hots for him?" Naël gave me the stink eye, so I amended, "I mean, do you like him?" The way she avoided my eyes told me all I needed to know. "Holy mackerel, you *do* have a crush on him. Honey, he's like —" I searched for a number but my mind couldn't quite wrap itself around it. "Hundreds of years older than you."

The young mermaid crossed her arms and pouted. "Age is just a number," she quoted. "Love crosses all barriers." Man, she had been hitting the Internet for platitudes, hadn't she?

Naël dropped his shopping bags on the floor and draped his arm over her shoulders. "However true that might be, Vee, I'm not sure Taz would be very happy."

"Taz is cool. She wouldn't stand in the way of true love," Vee said, stubbornly resisting her brother's pull.

"She liked Aiden but she never hated you for stealing him away from her."

I almost choked on a laugh. The child was either very innocent or possibly delusional—not sure which. There was no point in contradicting her, so I let it go, setting the bag with the books on top of the chair by the front door and walking into the kitchen where everyone was congregating.

"Who invited you all?" I asked. Besides Cristina, who had been asked to watch Vee while we shopped, Taz, Oisin, and Silva were all making themselves comfortable with our food.

"I did," Vee replied, grabbing an orange from the fruit bowl. "We need to discuss your wedding."

I swear the house rocked around me. "*My* wedding?" My voice came out a bit too screechy. "What makes you think I need you all to plan my wedding?" The thought was truly terrifying.

"Well, have you chosen a venue yet?" the young mermaid said, sounding more like a mother than a child.

No, I hadn't, but there was plenty of time. We weren't getting married until Christmas. That was a whole—shit! Only three weeks away.

"Vee is right about that, Aiden," Taz interjected unnecessarily. Fueling Vee's crazy ideas about my wedding was not wise or welcomed. "You have any idea of how hard it is to secure a venue for a wedding, especially this time of the year?"

I opened my mouth to protest, but my merrow spoke first. "They have a point, sweetheart. Maybe we should start looking." Not my sexy merman too. This was looking more and more like a conspiracy.

"There is a great place on the beach just down the road from us," Cristina offered, her index finger in her mouth. "It's called Coconuts by the Sea."

I knew the place. It was lovely, open and breezy, right by the ocean, but commercial—not us at all. Not to mention, I was so not willing to spend a fortune. Naël might be independently wealthy, but I was not going to spend his money to put on a show we didn't need.

Vee clapped her hands and bounced like a jack rabbit. "Yes! We can set up a wedding harbor with rainbow veils and topped with a unicorn horn."

I did choke then. Taz laughed—the wicked witch —and slapped me not-so-gently in the back. "Great idea, Vee," she added with a wink. "We could also cover all the chairs in fake mermaid scale fabric. It'd look lovely." If I wasn't coughing so much, I would have wrapped my hands around the witch's neck and squeezed until her eyes bugged out. Not enough to kill but just enough to make her life flash before her eyes.

Fouchard stepped closer and placed a protective arm over my shoulders. "I think Aiden is having a hard time with all of this," he said, laughter ill-disguised in his voice. "Let's just table this matter for now and come back to it after we have a chance to talk about it, okay?"

Surprisingly enough, it was Silva who stepped forward and said, "Absolutely. It's your wedding, not ours. Maybe you want to think of a place that means something special to both of you."

Now, why had I not thought of that myself?

Cristina looked like a chipmunk with a hoarding problem, her cheeks so puffed up with *travesseiros*; I was in wonder of how she could still mutter sounds. The soft, flaky pastries they called pillows were hot off the oven and onto our plates as we sat at the Piriquita, the famous coffee shop guilty of such sinful edible temptations. Even at the height of winter, the place was a mad house with people standing, sitting, and hanging over the long counter drinking coffee to wash down all that sugary goodness.

"I can't believe I managed to convince you to come to Sintra, my friend," Cristina said after swallowing her food. "A few months ago, you wouldn't even consider coming here."

"A few months ago, I had nothing but bad things to say about magicals and no reason to expose myself to the high magical traffic of this town." I had come a long way from hating my own kind to not only accepting but making friends with all sorts of magical creatures. I was, after all, one of them.

"Don't sell yourself short, amigo," she said, taking another huge bite off the pastry. She chewed a few times before continuing, "You used to be terrified of coming anywhere near Sintra."

"Well, the King of the Sexual Perverts no longer rules around here," I said. "It would be a waste not to visit this beautiful place."

It was gorgeous, and I had always been upset it was also Magical Grand Station. The micro-climate had long been favored by monarchy, poets, and celebrities to escape the heat of the summer and the harsh reality of modern life. This was a green heaven, heavy with wildlife, fresh water, history, and magic. Palaces peppered the *serra,* topped spectacularly by a gray Moorish castle, its crenellated walls undulating over the dips and rises of the rocky terrain.

"Perfect for a wedding," Cristina said and winked at me.

Naël and I had discussed it the night before and the Quinta da Regaleira had come up. The Quinta was where we had first made love, so what could be more perfect to stage our union? Cristina had offered to drive me there since our coffee shop was closed on Mondays and my mate had taken Vee to a school play audition.

"Wipe all that sugar from your face and let's go," I told my pregnant friend, who was working on her second pastry. How could she eat that much and stay so thin? Was that baby of hers sucking up all the calories? "Since we are not sneaking in at night like we normally do, we need to get to the gate before they close."

We dropped a tip on the sugar-covered tabletop and left the coffee shop. I stood for a few seconds contemplating the steep climb up to the Quinta. After a long inhale, I let out a loud breath and started the hike up the mountain, Cristina in tow.

It was strange to walk in the place through the front gate. In the past, we had always stolen our way into the grounds by either climbing the lowest walls or teleporting to the other side, using my coolest magical talent—at least in my humble opinion. I wanted to check out the chapel, under which Naël and I had been intimate for the first time. Not the most romantic or comfortable of sites, but it kept us away from the eyes of the Virgin Mary in the painting over the altar. I was not religious at all, but the chapel was a beautiful example of neo-Manueline architecture and would most definitely be a great venue for a wedding.

We paid ten euros each for our tickets and made our way up the hill to where the path was lined by life-size statues of a variety of gods and goddesses. I was a bit ambivalent about this; I was the son of a goddess—an amazing woman if I may say so myself—but I had also been chased and almost killed by a god, however ridiculous. So, my respect for their divinity was a little iffy at best.

As soon as we turned the corner in the path and faced the pretty white structure of the chapel, now decorated with evergreens and red baubles, memories came flooding in. My pants began shrinking as images of that kiss sandwiched between my merrow and the cold interior wall of the chapel took over all my senses. I could still feel the warmth of his lips on mine, his taste on my tongue, his hard body against mine....

But then, just as quickly, memories of another kind came rushing in: the way the depraved King of the Folk made me feel, the way he ran his hands over my lover's body, and the way Naël had been trussed up like a turkey and anchored at the bottom of a soft-water pond.

I shook my head like a wet dog, and Cristina threw me one of her are-you-losing-your-mind looks. "That's not the way to get rid of lice, in case you didn't know." I'll say it again; with friends like mine, who needed enemies? "What's wrong with you?"

"This is not the place." My blood froze and I shivered.

"What do you mean? This is the only chapel in the Quinta." Cristina frowned, her eyebrows knitted so tightly they might as well be a unibrow.

I hugged myself, trying to chase some of the cold away. "I mean, this is not right for our wedding," I explained, my teeth clicking rapidly like castanets in a flamenco dance. "Too many bad memories here. No, scratch this venue off the list."

I turned around to leave, but my friend grabbed my arm. "Are you okay?" Sweet Cristina was back.

I smiled at her. "I'm fine," I lied. "Let's not come back here for a long while, okay?" She nodded and, hooking her arm on mine, walked in silence down the path with me.

I guess I needed more time to heal from a few things after all.

CHAPTER 2

Jingle Goats

"Earth to Major Aiden." Taz, all red hair and crazy sunglasses, stood before me, half bent so her face was smack in front of mine, her scarlet lips puckered in mock worry. "Geez, Aiden, where the hell did you go for the past few minutes?"

Bringing my mind back to reality from wherever it had gone, I flattened my hand on her face and pushed her away from me. "Stay away, witch. I forgot my garlic."

She slapped my hand away and frowned, straightening the sunglasses on her nose and rubbing her lips together. "Fuck! I'm not a vampire, idiot. Now you smudged my lipstick."

"Serves you right for not respecting my personal

space." I sounded like a child even to my own ears. I had been so preoccupied with figuring out where to hold our wedding, I had been a pain in everybody's ass—including my own. "Be a good witch and get me a *bica*, will you?"

Before the witch could explode—and she most certainly would—my soul mate came to her rescue with two cups of hot espresso and a truffle.

"No need to kill each other," he said in that sexy voice of his. "Remember, it's Christmastime, a time for tolerance and goodwill to men—and women," he rushed to add before Taz took exception. "But in our case, goodwill to this man in particular." He wagged his eyebrows in a very Marx Brothers' way and I had to laugh. My usually stern and cantankerous merman could be very funny sometimes.

I pulled him against my side and squeezed his delicious ass. "Oh, I will most definitely show you a boatload of goodwill later, my sweet merrow." He chuckled and bent down to kiss the top of my head. "I just can't come up with an idea for a wedding venue that doesn't reek of bad memories. It's driving me nuts."

"You mean nuttier, right?" Taz interjected, daintily sticking out her pinky finger as she took the coffee to her lips. "Because you are already a nut."

I gave her the stink eye and then took a swig of the

hot coffee. "What do you think of the Capuchos Convent? We could have the ceremony out in the courtyard at night." We had had such great moments together in that place, it made sense to hold it there.

"That's a great idea," my man said, glancing at the clock on the wall, a beautiful kitschy thing I had recently purchased from a local store. "Shit. I promised Vee I would be there for the first rehearsal. Can you check it out for me, sweetheart?"

Disappointment must have been obvious on my face because Taz leaned forward over the table and said, "Oh, don't be so sad, Aiden. I'll go with you."

I snorted. "Like I need your company." But I did. I hadn't been to the convent since Fouchard had surprised me with a private birthday celebration in the fall. I hated to go there without my lover. Then, there was my dad, my druid-monk father who lived a humble life in the convent. I wondered what my mom thought about that. And did I want to see him again so soon? I had forgiven him for abandoning me as a babe, but there was still some anger inside me. "What time do you want to go?" I might as well give in.

Taz screeched. "Give me a minute to fix my make-up." Like the monks would care what she looked like.

I watched her walk to the bathroom and then turned to Naël. "You owe me big. Now I have to go to the convent with Taz, the teenage-like witch. God, give me patience."

Naël planted another kiss on my head, ruffled my hair with a big hand, and laughed. "I will make sure you are well rewarded for your sacrifice, sweetheart. Tonight, after rehearsal." Whoosh, my pants shrank a few sizes at the promise in his voice. I followed him with hungry eyes as he left the coffee shop to go meet with his sister. I sighed.

"Did I hear that correctly?" It was Cristina, tray in one hand and towel on the other. "You're going to Capuchos with Taz?"

I nodded, resigned to my fate. "If you were a good friend, you'd come too." I knew she couldn't. As my one and only employee, she couldn't possibly abandon her post. We both needed the money and the coffee shop was open until nine in the winter. "Say a little prayer for me, will you?"

There had been a time when Taz and I were like oil and water except much more belligerent. We were like two betta fish in the same tank. As much as I hated to admit it though, she had become a good friend, the only one I had that was on board with my love for pop culture and often the only one who got my cheesy jokes. That didn't mean I would let her know.

The Convento dos Capuchos was located in Sintra

too, higher in the mountain and away from the eyes of the public. During the day it was a tourist attraction, open to everyone and normally crowded, but at night it was a different story. As soon as the place closed its gates to the public, a wall of trees and vegetation grew around it, blocking it from view and protecting the magic druids who lived within. I had spent many days and nights in the convent, first alone and then with my merman. Even Vee had stayed with us once.

Brother John was waiting for us in the parking lot. He had exchanged his usual brown habit for mundane clothes so he could blend in with the few tourists that had dared to face the cold of winter to visit the place and were slowly returning to their cars as the convent closed for the evening. His white hair was now short, but his eyes were still much the same blue as mine.

"Well, hello, Father," I said, unable to hide the slight touch of bitterness in my voice. "Since when did you join the welcome committee?"

Taz slapped my arm with a loud sheesh. My father chuckled. "I will always be here to welcome you, son," he said. "We spent way too many years apart, and I'm not getting any younger."

I bit my tongue so I wouldn't utter the words trying to come out—*and whose fault was that?* "You got my message then?" I had called the convent and left the usual coded message that warned the monks of my impending visit. After my run-in with their horrifying latrines, the Oracle had thought it would be funny if I was to leave a message in the ticket office complaining about the toilets. I failed to find the humor in it, but who was I to deny a very old kook his fun?

My father nodded, and we all began the long walk to the main courtyard with a short stop in the tourist bathrooms. I didn't want to run the risk of having to use the previously mentioned latrines.

As usual, the whole brotherhood was waiting in the small refectory, sat around the rustic slab of stone that served as a table. The delicious smell of food hit my nostrils as soon as we walked up the couple steps and made my mouth water. If there was one thing these monks were good at, it was cooking. Their cooking was simple but delicious and generous in quantity.

A cacophony of voices assailed us when the monks rose from their seats to greet us. "Man, didn't realize you were so popular around here," Taz muttered, her eyes as big as full moons. "I feel I should light you a candle or something."

"I take cash," I whispered back as I went around shaking everyone's hands. I would never admit it, but it was heartwarming to be welcomed like that, for a loner and outcast like I had been my whole life. "Let's eat, people." I couldn't take much of this adoring crowd. Tears were already burning in my eyes. One more pat on the back and I would burst out crying like a widow at a funeral.

We all sat around the table and ate until our stomachs were fighting the table for space. "Damn, this food is good." Taz covered her mouth in obvious distress. "Shit, I'm sorry... dang, cursed again. Sorry, sorry...."

Brother John, aka my dad, shrugged. "Don't worry, Ms. Maloid; we monks are not prudish." The witch had a last name? And how did my father know that? "After all, we are druids."

Taz's red lips stretched into a mischievous smile. "Does that mean you have beer in your fridge?"

My father laughed while I still struggled with the fact Taz had a last name I had never known. "Well, not in the fridge, because we don't have one, but yes, we have ale if that will do."

I had never seen Taz so excited about booze. *Apparently, witches love ale. Go figure!*

I left her drinking what she had left of her wits with the monks and walked across the courtyard to check out the place. I didn't remember a full moon when we first arrived, but there it was, round and white like a big wheel of cheese—if cheese could actually hang in space. I walked around to the back to the smaller, quieter courtyard where Vee had taken a bath in the fountain and traumatized the poor goldfish living in it. It was still as beautiful as I remembered, and the nature around it made me feel stronger and revitalized.

But something felt wrong. Not wrong as in the actual place, but wrong as the setting for our wedding.

"Fuck, can you be any pickier, Aiden?" I yelled out into the night.

"They say speaking to yourself in the second person is the first sign of madness." My father had sneaked up behind me and stood with his arms crossed and legs apart. Being a tall man in jeans and a plaid shirt, he could easily pass for a lumberjack. I held back a chuckle. "What are you doing here alone?"

"Trying to decide whether this is the right place for my wedding." It was no secret why I was in the convent. "Something feels weird."

We stood side by side in silence, staring at the moon. "Come," my father eventually said. "Let's go see the Oracle."

"What? Is he sane at the moment?" With him you never knew. Of course, it could also be that weird drink he always slurped on.

Brother John laughed. "He is a lot saner than you think. Maybe he can help you decide whether to hold the ceremony here."

I had to admit, I kind of missed the crazy old man. As quirky—code word for totally nuts—as he was, I had grown to like him. He had helped me find my parents after all and given me and Fouchard shelter when we needed to lie low for a while. Not sure how much he could help with the current issue, but I was not against seeing him again. So, I followed my father in the direction of the library where the old kook lived.

Before walking in, my father stopped me. "Word of warning, don't drink anything he offers you."

"Why?" I had indeed accepted a drink from him before.

"Just trust your father for once," he said, walking into the building. "That is if you want to keep your wits about you and your stomach inside you."

Well, alrighty then!

It had been a couple months since I'd seen the old cuckoo Einstein look-alike. He hadn't changed a bit. I found him exactly on the same spot I had seen him the last time I visited, eyes closed and white hair standing on end as if he had never learned how to use a brush.

"It's about time you came for a visit, Aiden." The old man never opened his eyes as we walked in. "Take a seat," he said, pointing at a cushion on the floor in front of the mattress he apparently lived on.

At closer inspection, I knew it was the same cushion he had offered months ago—a definite improvement from sitting on the cold stone floor but still old, ratty, and far from comfortable.

"Remind me to bring my own cushion next time," I whispered to my old man as I slumped down to the floor and crossed my legs. "How have you been, Brother Serafim? Long time no see."

"Cut the crap, young man," he said, still with his eyes closed. "You're not here to inquire about my health."

I wasn't, but I could be polite when I wanted to. "Yes, I came to Capuchos to figure out whether I wanted to hold my wedding here."

A younger brother walked in, a tray in his hands. He put it down on the only table in the room, poured something from the bottle into an old ceramic mug, and handed it to the Oracle. I watched the seer with interest as he took tiny sips from the cup, sighing after each one.

"You don't want to hold it here, trust me." The old man finally opened his eyes, too bright for a man of his age. Not that I had any idea of how old he was, but I would guess a couple hundred years old. Okay, maybe I was exaggerating, but he was indeed very old.

"Why not?" The fact that my instincts were telling me the same exact thing didn't stop me from questioning his word. "It's beautiful; Naël and I had some great times here."

A low chuckle escaped the Oracle's thin lips. "Yes, I should say you had." Monks and their freakish modern monitoring system. I had forgotten he had seen us together a few times. "Yet, I am certain you know this wouldn't be the right place for it."

I let out a loud exhale. I couldn't deny my feelings. "You're right, I do." God, I hated to admit he was right. "It's too restrictive," I explained, finally pinpointing the reason. The convent didn't allow everyone in. In fact, only those related to the druid monks had access to it after hours. In theory I could invite as many people as I wanted, but did I really wish to ruin the convent's layer of mystery just to hold my wedding? Wouldn't that in essence ruin the beautiful memories we had made there? "We wouldn't be able to invite all our friends and I think I want to keep Capuchos our little secret anyway."

"Wherever you decide, maybe we can hold a feast here afterward," the Oracle said, after another sip of the mystery drink. "The brothers would be excited to have you."

Having the monks cook for us on our wedding day? Fuck yeah! I was so on board with that. "That's very generous of you, Brother Serafim. I'm sure Fouchard would love that."

Yet another young monk walked in, his head bowed. "Sorry to interrupt, but your friend, the witch, is turning the courtyard bushes into bunnies."

I rolled my eyes. If she couldn't hold her liquor, why drink so much? "I knew it was a mistake to bring her with me," I mumbled, scrambling to my feet. "Sorry, I have to make sure she doesn't start stripping in front of the brothers." Even though, gods knew, these guys needed a little entertainment.

My father and I hurried to where Taz, drunk as a skunk, was—like the monk had said—turning every bush into giant, fluffy rabbits. I shook my head and sighed. "Holy Mother of God, Taz," I exclaimed loud enough to be heard in England. "Can I not leave for a second without you turning into *Buffy*'s Anya?"

Taz whipped her red mane—her bun had vanished and her hair now fell in loose curls in front of her face —around and pointed a finger at me. "Ah, shows how much you know, Aiden. Anya was scared of bunnies. I, on the other hand, *love* them." She actually cackled.

I held her by both shoulders and made her look at me. "Witch, turn those bunnies back to their real form. Now."

She humphed, stumbled a bit, and waved her hand in the air. "You're such a humbug. What's so great about bushes?"

I stole a glance at the hopping creatures, which were quickly turning back into vegetation. "The monks need those bushes for a variety of things. Nothing grows in the convent that is not used for something." I turned my head to my father, who was having way too much fun watching the whole scene. "I think it's time to take Ms. Maloid home, don't you agree?"

Brother John nodded, an amused smile still dancing on his lips. "I will help you to the car, son."

Between the two of us, we were able to drag a now-barefooted Taz to where the car was parked just outside the wall of magic and secure her to the passenger seat with the seatbelt.

"This is my car." She slurred her speech and could hardly keep her eyes open. "Shit! What do the monks put in that ale?"

I chuckled, sliding beside her in the driver's seat.

"Probably the same thing Brother Serafim drinks." Before I closed the door, I glanced at my father. "Thank you," I said, leaving it open to interpretation. Was I thanking him for today or for being back in my life? Hopefully he knew because I sure didn't.

I shut the door, waved, and drove the car out of the parking spot and onto the main road. I wondered if my mother would agree to holding the wedding in Obidos? A honeymoon night in that same room we had slept—well, there hadn't been much sleep involved —in the spring would be amazing.

I was starting to enjoy having parents in high places. A druid father and a goddess mother were nothing to be sneezed at after all.

Note to self: avoid drunk witches. Unlike other drunkards, witches tend to turn random objects into even more random things in their drunken stupor. Turns out it is very hard to drive on winding, narrow roads with jumping dwarf goats bleating like banshees in the back seat.

I left Taz in her own bed, after I used a tiny portion of my healing powers to put her to sleep so she wouldn't turn her apartment into a petting zoo, threw her car keys on the kitchen counter, and wished myself home. I was getting more and more attached to this gift of mine; teleporting was very convenient indeed and saved me a ton of money on Uber rides.

It was way past midnight and everyone in the house must have been asleep because nothing was stirring. *Not even a mouse.* I chuckled to myself; Christmas season was obviously having some strange effect on me. I grabbed a bottle of water from the fridge, gulped it down in one go, and then went upstairs to our room.

Naël was not in bed.

Shivers of alarm ran through my body. Where was my merman? He wasn't downstairs either—I'd checked. Quietly and trying to keep my rising panic from taking control, I cracked Vee's room door just enough to confirm she was fast asleep in her bed. So where was my merrow?

Slipping my phone off my pocket, I quickly speed-dialed Fouchard's number. He picked up right away. "Where the hell are you?" I asked, much louder than I intended.

"Shh, you'll wake up Vee," he said, infuriatingly calm while my heart was going a thousand miles a minute. "Why are you so upset?"

"Shit, Naël. I thought you—" I couldn't say it out loud for fear it would actually happen. After all the events of the past year, anything could send me into panic mode. I took a deep breath before responding, "I was worried when I didn't see you in the room."

Fouchard chuckled softly. "Idiot." Yeah, that was my man all right. "I have a surprise for you. You would know if you checked your messages once in a while."

I pulled away from the phone to check the text messages, and sure enough, there it was. "It must have come in while I was driving the crazy witch home," I said. "Hard to hear anything with a couple of goats in the back."

"Goats? Why did you have goats in the car?" I sighed, not quite ready to tell him the whole sordid story of Taz, the Lush. "Never mind, you can tell me later. Come to the beach."

Without bothering to end the call, I pocketed the phone and rushed down to the underground beach. The soft moonlight-imitating lamps along the top of the high rock walls were all lit and I could see Fouchard sitting on the sand not too far from the water. He waved as soon as he saw me.

"Finally," he said as I dropped down to the sand in front of him. "I thought I'd have to eat all of this by myself."

Spread on top of a red-checkered cloth, Fouchard had a small but delicious-looking array of foods. All my favorites were there: *pasteis de nata, rissóis de camarão, bolas de Berlim* and even a plate of *caracois.* He knew me well.

"What's the occasion?" I asked, salivating like a puppy over a bone.

"I felt guilty not being able to help you much with the venue search, so I hoped to make it up to you by filling your belly." He had a wicked smile on his lips. "Just don't eat too much, because dessert will require some bending." He winked and I just about lost it.

I stuffed a pastel in my mouth and pushed him down to the sand, melting my body to his. I tried to kiss him but belatedly realized my miscalculation; my mouth was busy with the pastry. He laughed and waited while I half chewed, half swallowed it, his hands on either side of my waist, fingers sneaking underneath my shirt.

"Well, Mr. Mercer, are you trying to eat your dessert before the main course?" Both his hands were now firmly on my butt and pressing me against his hardness.

"You know how Pinocchio gets," I quipped, trailing kisses along his jaw. "I have to attend to his needs first. Then I'll eat."

It wasn't going to take long to strip him of his clothes; he wasn't wearing much besides a pair of jeans and a T-shirt. I pulled the shirt off first, then peppered kisses along his chest and down to his rock-hard stomach. He lifted his head from the sand to watch me, as I wasted no time unzipping his pants and pulling them down his hips.

No underwear. Perfect.

I went down on him even before I had finished pulling down his pants. I could never get enough of my merman's taste, a mixture of ocean and sunshine. He grunted, arching against my mouth while my tongue performed its magic. I slipped my hands beneath him and kneaded his perfectly firm ass. We had come a long way since we first met; the barbs still surfaced but now they held a much more intimate, loving meaning. I knew my merman, he knew me, and we both knew the true meaning behind our sarcastic bickering. Let others think what they will.

Fouchard let out such a loud groan as I dragged my lips over and away from his velvety skin, I was afraid Vee might hear it. "Ready?" He nodded emphatically and shuffled a little on the sand, legs still trapped by his jeans, to grab a bottle of lube from the checkered blanket. While he fiddled with the cover, I freed him from his pants and soon we were both well-oiled and fit to be fried.

"Turn over." My beautiful hot merrow complied,

exposing that sweet ass of his to my greedy eyes and other body parts. "You sexy merman," I whispered, running a finger between his butt cheeks. "I'm going to take you to heaven and back."

I heard a muffled chuckle. "Promises, promises," my lover said. "But can you put your money where your mouth is?"

It was my turn to snort. "Oh, sweetheart, I can do something so much better than that."

And I did.

CHAPTER 3

Tails We've Heard on High

I looked around me for something sharp I could poke my eyes out with. Walking in on Taz making out with the ginger god, Oisin, was enough to traumatize me for life.

"For all that's sacred, Taz!" I yelled, covering my eyes with my arm. "Not in my house."

"Give it a rest, magic boy," Taz retorted with her usual aplomb. Blinded by my own arm, I heard shuffling of feet and zipping of pants. "This is technically your merman's house, not yours."

Low blow, Taz. "We are a unit so all that's his is mine, and all that's mine is his." Cheesy, I knew and, considering I didn't own much, a little unbalanced too. "You have a house and Oisin..." Hell, where did the god live exactly?

"I apologize, Aiden," Oisin said, his voice too deep for the age he appeared to be. "We got a little carried away."

I'll say! When I deemed it safe to uncover my eyes, I noticed the tabletop lamp on its side, knick-knacks strewed across the carpet, and even a picture that had been previously hanging on the wall now lying face-down on the floor. *A little carried away?*

Oisin followed my gaze. "Oh, shit. Sorry," he said, waving a hand in the direction of the mess. Even after a whole lifetime of experience with magicals, I was still shocked to watch him manipulate all the fallen objects into place with just a gesture. The room was back to its former, tidy glory in a wink of an eye. "There, fixed."

"I would suggest you get a room, but you already have one that obviously does not meet your kinky needs." Yes, I was being totally hypocritical. Fouchard and I had made love in so many inappropriate spots, and yet, here I was preaching against it. "What are you doing here anyway? Have you ever heard of knocking or calling ahead?" Now that Taz had been invited into our house, there was no way of stopping the witch from popping out of nowhere any time she wanted.

"For your information, we were invited by Naël." *Really? Why?* "He told us you needed help."

I snorted. "From you guys? I don't need any bunnies or goats in my wedding."

Taz scrunched up her pretty face and crossed her arms over her generous bosom. "May I remind you of who was with you when you visited the King of the Fae? Or when you rescued Fouchard from the grotto? Or who took care of you when you were hit by the *brahmachakram*?" She puckered her lips in a perfect imitation of Zoolander and almost made me laugh. "Me. That would be me."

All true, but Taz and I had a long history of not giving each other credit. That's how our friendship rolled. And yes, I had long admitted to myself—if not to others—that we were indeed friends. It was so much more fun to act as if we were not though.

"Have you recovered completely from your drunken stupor?" I asked with just enough bitchiness to make her mad. Not that anything ever got the little witch upset. She seemed to have an inexhaustible tolerance for sarcasm.

"It's been a week, Aiden, but thanks for asking." Yep, nothing pissed her off. "Have you decided on a wedding venue yet?"

Fuck no. Every time I thought I had it, some dark memory ruined it for me. After talking to my mom about maybe holding it at the castle in Obidos, I remembered that we were there when we got the news of Vee's kidnapping. I doubted if Fouchard would ever be able to visit the place without flashbacks to that terrible time. I wouldn't want my mate to go through that again.

I shook my head. "Still thinking about it. What's going on with the two of you, getting all hot and heavy?" I was a master at deflecting.

"Of all people, Aiden, you should understand how it feels to find the one," Oisin said so deadpan I almost believed him.

Taz's pretty face just melted—and not in a Wicked Witch of the West fashion. "Aww, Oisin, that's so sweet. I feel the same." Wait! What? They actually meant it?

"When did this... " I searched for words to express my utter shock and disbelief. "This *romance* thing happen?" Obviously, they had been playing footsie almost since the day they'd met back in the summer when we had the showdown with Bob, the Idiot God. But this lovey-dovey-you're-the-one crap? That was new to me.

The witch circled the ginger god's waist with her arm and pulled him against her. "You would know if you ever got your head out of your ass." Have I mentioned I sometimes have trouble telling my friends apart from my enemies? "We've been dating for ages now." If *ages* were actually a couple months, I guess. She peered at me, her perfectly made-up lashes fluttering. "Are you jealous, Aiden? You had your chance." *As if.*

"Keep dreaming, witch," I said, plopping a pod in the coffee machine by the window. "I have my man." And what a man he was. Just thinking about him melted my skivvies. "Did you have a reason to invade my home other than to make out with your god?"

She let go of said god and dropped to the nearest couch. Oisin perched on the arm of the sofa, curiosity and amusement twinkling in his pale blue eyes. "I'm serious. We're here to help you in your search." Taz clicked her tongue. "You might be good at finding missing people or sniffing out murderers, but you obviously suck at nailing a wedding venue."

I wasn't going to admit that she might be on to something. Not even to myself. "And you are?"

She straightened her back, raised her carefully manicured eyebrows, and puckered her lips. "Of course I am." So humble. "I even made a list." Shit! Maybe she was actually good at it.

With a comical smile, Taz patted the seat next to her and winked at me. I shook my head and sighed. What was I going to do with her? One minute I wanted to strangle her, the next I considered kissing her. Maybe just a quick peck on the cheek. *Wait! Scratch that.* Maybe just a high-five.

"All right, witch, let's get on with it." If you can't beat them, make them work for you, I always say.

* * *

I was in the middle of my second-favorite exercise routine—having sex with Naël being the first—when Vee sneaked behind me and just about made my heart jump out of my mouth. "Child, one of these days you will kill me," I exclaimed, panting like a dog on a hot day. "Don't you see I am exercising?"

Vee's eyes narrowed and her eyebrows knitted together. "Exercising? You're watching my brother swim."

Shit! I couldn't tell a twelve-year-old that watching my merman flap his beautiful blue tail made certain muscles in my body flex and my heart gallop.

"I'm exercising my eyes," I said instead, a frog in my throat. "What are you doing here, little mermaid?"

She dropped to the sand beside me, crossed her legs, and braced her elbows on her knees, her lips stretched into a pout. "You haven't accepted any of my suggestions for your wedding." Oh crap, she had finally caught on. "Why do you hate me so much?"

"Oh, for all that's holy, girl." She was such a drama queen sometimes. "Why would I hate my boyfriend's sister? And such a cute one at that. Look at all those curls." Her almost-white hair was a mess as usual, but it somehow fitted her perfectly. The profusion of wild curls and kinks framed a pretty, however impish amber face. Her freckles covered her upper cheeks and the bridge of her tiny, upturned nose, and her pink lips crumpled into a frown. "I'm just not a big fan of unicorns."

That was not going to fly.

"But unicorns are unique, like you and my brother," she argued, her green eyes twinkling. Gah, the girl knew how to work it. "Why wouldn't you want some in your wedding?"

I sighed. Loudly. "Vee, I promise that I will try really hard to include unicorns into our wedding ceremony, okay?" There was no arguing with that mermaid. "But first I have to find a place to hold it in, don't you think?"

"What about St. George's Castle?" she said, her frown dissipating. "Your mom would definitely let you hold it there. She probably could close the whole place up just for you." Considering she was a goddess, that was probably true. My mother would do that for me if I asked her, and the castle where her restaurant and main residence were located was beautiful, perched on top of Lisbon's highest hill, overlooking the city and the river Tagus. But it still did not feel right.

Yes, I was now all about the feels. When had I become so sappy?

"No, not the castle either," I said, hating myself for all the indecision. "Got to be special and mean nothing but happy memories."

Vee clicked her tongue like an old woman. "Man, you're complicated, Aiden. If you don't decide soon, you may end up getting married in our garden." She was right. Even with all my friends' magical powers put together, it would still warrant a miracle to find a wedding venue that close to the date and during Christmas season.

All my troubling thoughts suddenly ran out of me as I watched my fiancé emerge from the surf, water sliding and dripping from every inch of his sexy, dark skin, rivulets curling around his hard pecs and meandering down to his stone abs and—damn, he was wearing swim trunks this time. Still, I could easily imagine, couldn't I?

"What's the fuss about?" he asked, picking up a blue towel from our bag and wrapping himself tightly with it. *Merman sushi. Yum.* "You both looked a bit agitated."

Vee clicked her tongue again. "He can't decide on —" I snapped to my knees and covered her mouth with a hand. Furious, she tried to bite me. *Brat!*

Fouchard gave me a look and I shrugged. "I'm trying to decide on a wedding gift for you so I don't want her to spoil the surprise." Man, I was getting good at lying. He seemed to believe me and shook his head, droplets of salty water flying in every direction. I licked the one that fell on my lips and moaned a bit, trollop that I was. "Are we still going out for ice cream?"

My mate's forehead furrowed. "Are you kidding me? It's winter." It was like sixty degrees outside, hardly what I would call cold.

Vee came to the rescue. "The Italian creamery is open all year. Don't be a wimp, Naël. Let's go for ice cream." Her lip extended out a good inch and a half, a weapon of mass persuasion against her brother.

He closed his eyes for a moment and I knew he had surrendered. With a dramatic sigh, he said, "All right, let me go get dressed." And he left the subterranean beach to me and the little imp.

The freckled mermaid offered me a wide grin, her arms crossed over her chest. "See? Got to know how to work it," she gloated. "You need to find the cracks in my brother's armor and attack through them."

That girl was too much. Cracks? Armor? Where did she learn that? Probably from her mermaid friends who seemed to be overly mature for their tween years.

Soon we were all sitting outside the festive creamery, licking giant balls of Italian ice cream while being whipped by a chilly breeze. It would have been strangely erotic were an eleven-year-old not sitting between me and my man. Still, I couldn't help stealing hot glances at my merman, who seemed totally oblivious that I was undressing him in my mind.

"Odd choice for a cold day." Silva, the outrageously handsome warlock cop, stood a few feet away from us, one perfect dark eyebrow raised and legs braced shoulder-length apart. "Or do merfolk not feel cold like others do?"

Before Fouchard could answer, I jumped in, snark in hand. "Apparently warlocks are not as tough as they say they are. I wonder what Cristina would do if she found out her fiancé is a wimp." I would keep the fact I was chilled to the bone to myself.

Infuriatingly, the man burst out laughing. "Oh, Mercer, you are getting funnier and funnier with each passing day. Or is it naive?"

I had never been called that and wasn't sure how I

felt about it. So, like the ten-year-old that lived inside me, I crossed my arms tightly and humphed. Silva laughed again and the amused glint in Fouchard's eyes told me he was laughing inside too.

"Sit, Silva," my boyfriend said, gesturing toward a stool. "Want some ice cream?"

"Gods, no. I like warmth." Silva pulled one of the free stools closer to the table and sat down. "I have something for you, Mercer," he said. "A case."

I shook my head so fiercely, the world danced before my eyes. "No, no. I told you I am done with detective work. I just want to drink coffee and sunbathe from now on." And make hot, sweet love to my merrow. I was a simple man with simple needs.

"This is nothing dangerous," the cop protested, leaning in over the tabletop. "A simple missing item case. No murder, no blood and guts, no danger."

"What's missing?" My not-so-helpful sister-in-law asked, a big blob of ice cream decorating her upper lip.

"A merman tail."

My blood froze in my veins. "What? I thought we got rid of the poachers," I managed to say through the huge lump in my throat.

Silva raised an appeasing hand. "Calm down, man. Not a real tail." Was I hearing him correctly or did my many dips in a cold ocean damage my hearing? He stuck a hand in his shirt pocket, searching for something. "I have a picture somewhere. It was a commissioned work by a silicone artist, worth quite a bit of money."

I raised an eyebrow, my blood thawing out. "There is such a thing as fake tails?"

"Where have you been, Aiden?" my little sister-in-law to be piped in. Cheeky monkey. "Merfolk stuff is in crazy demand."

I rolled my eyes. "Like you'd know." Yes, it was hard for me to act like a grownup when around the little imp. She ignored me.

"Behave, you two," my merrow said, amusement dancing in his eyes and voice. "So, someone stole it?"

"More like tailnapped it," the warlock said, producing a folded photo out of his wallet. "Here." He handed it to me. "They want the artist to pay an exorbitant amount of money for it, and even though it is worth quite a bit, it's definitely not worth that." I unfolded the piece of paper and studied the picture of a gorgeous silicone merman tail. The details were exquisite and the colors mesmerizing. "The owner is offering a hefty reward to anyone who finds it."

I squinted at the warlock cop. "Why don't you find it yourself?" I smelled something fishy, and I didn't mean my lovely merman.

"Because I have bigger fish to fry—no pun intended." The subtle upturn of his lips told me otherwise. "I thought you might be happy to get a few extra bucks to help with the planning of your wedding."

I stole a glance at my mate and he nodded. "Might as well, Aiden. Might keep your mind off the wedding."

"But who will find the venue?" Vee perked up and I extended a hand to stop her. "No, Vee. I love you but you will not be in charge of finding a venue. You are far too young for that."

"Aiden is right, Vee," Fouchard said. "I will help you, sweetheart, when I can, and I'm sure Taz and Cristina will also lend a hand." I was itching for a good mystery, not that I'd admit it even to myself. "Who knows? Maybe you will be inspired by the case and think of a good place to hold the wedding in."

"Well? Will you take the challenge?" Silva probed me with his eyes, one corner of his mouth tipping upward.

I sighed, half annoyed with myself. "All right. I will do what I can."

Silva clapped his hands once and stood up. "Perfect. I will send you all the info I have by tonight. Now I must go see about a pretty regular." He meant my friend Cristina, who had been unwise enough to fall for the warlock and then, not happy enough, gotten herself pregnant with his baby. True, he had grown on me over the last few months but more like a weed rather than a beneficial plant. I still was not happy about the idea of my very non-magical friend dating someone as powerful as he was. Cristina still bore the scars of her last encounter with Bob, the Idiot God, only that had been all my fault.

My phone rang just as the cop walked away. Fouchard winked at me and I almost dropped the cell. "Make it quick," I told Taz at the other end. "I must take my fiancé home quickly." And make mad love to him.

"Isn't Vee with you? You're shameless, Aiden." She was one to talk, getting hot and heavy with the Irish god in our house. "I got you a wedding gift."

"Newsflash, witch, the wedding is not for a couple weeks." Secretly, I thought Taz's quirkiness to be rather charming most of the time, but I wouldn't admit it even under torture.

"It's an advance gift, idiot," she replied with a click of the tongue. "A night for you and your merman at the fabulous Palácio dos Arcos Hotel, all included."

My ears perked up. "Original building or the new section?" I was not the most gracious gift-receiver.

I could almost see Taz's eyes rolling. "Old building of course. I know how picky you are." She mumbled something under her breath that sounded a lot like an insult before continuing, "It's one of the few rooms in the old palace with a view of the ocean."

That sounded heavenly. "How did you swing that? I hear it's really hard to secure a room in the original building."

"I'm a witch," she said totally unhelpfully. "I have ways."

Bunch of bullshit. I told her as much. I bet she had got it through my mom who just happened to be her High Priestess and also a goddess. Dona Penelope owned a few hotels and restaurants around the country, so it would be pretty easy to do it.

"All right, party pooper," the witch exclaimed, her voice hitting a high note. "Your mother knows the owner. She wanted me to keep it a secret so it didn't look like she was trying to butt in your life."

"My mother is the only person allowed to butt in," I said and meant it. Despite the fact she and my father had abandoned me in a hostile non-magical world as a tiny kid, I didn't hold that against her. With my father it was different; I'm not sure why. "You, on the other hand, are not. I will call my mother and thank her for the gift."

"You're such an ungrateful mother—" I hung up before she could finish what she was saying. A satisfied smile crawled all the way to my lips as I put my cell phone back in my pocket.

"What did you do?" Fouchard asked, an eyebrow shooting up. "Why do you have to bicker with Taz all the time?"

"Because it's fun." One hundred percent true. I stood up, rubbed my arms, and said, "Come on, my love. We have some packing to do."

CHAPTER 4

Away in a First-Class Hotel

I scratched my head for the tenth time that afternoon. Could this be? It felt like too much of a coincidence that the first clue in the mertailnapping led me exactly to where Fouchard and I were going to spend the weekend. But then again, as I learned the hard way, my life was a pool of weirdness and unexpected revelations, so who knew?

"You're going to get a bald spot if you keep at it." Fouchard stole a glance in my direction before returning his attention to the road ahead.

I grunted. "Will you love me less if I do?" I slid my hands under my butt to keep them from moving again.

"Nuh, not possible," my sweet merman said. "As long as other parts of you are still in perfect working condition."

"So, you only love me for my sexual prowess, is that it?" Feigning anger, I tried to cross my arms over my chest only to realize they were stuck beneath my ass.

Fouchard snorted. "Well, I wouldn't go as far as using the word prowess, but you do have some skills." I shook my head, lips pursed in a very tween pout. The more I hung around Vee, the more mannerisms I picked up from her. My boyfriend laughed and slapped my thigh playfully. "Stop pouting. You know I love everything about you, even your tendency to make bad jokes."

"I don't tell bad jokes," I protested. "You're the one who doesn't get them." Taz was one of the few people I knew who always laughed at my jokes. Could she be my long-lost sister? *No, no, banish the thought.* I had no witches in my ancestry.

The hotel was less than twenty minutes down the road from Fouchard's house in Cascais. He parked the car in the quaint, fairy-lights-illuminated courtyard where a large fir stood, decorated with golden bows and sparkling baubles the size of soccer balls. The sun was far in its descent, painting the sky in a rainbow of beautiful colors that dipped into the choppy ocean. The view was amazing and soothing.

As soon as we crossed the main door into the lobby, a giraffe of a man came from behind the dark wood counter to greet us. "Bem vindos ao Palácio dos Arcos e feliz Natal." Thankfully my Portuguese was getting much better; otherwise, instead of knowing he was welcoming us, his enthusiasm and voice volume would make me think he was about to attack us.

"We have a reservation," my merrow said, a tiny smile on his lips. "Fouchard and Mercer."

The man tilted his absurdly long neck for a moment until recognition lit in his eyes. "Of course, I'm so sorry I didn't recognize you." Why would he? It wasn't as if we were celebrities. He lowered his voice and leaned in closer. "Mr. Mercer, you are a legend among our kind." *Fuck, a magical!* "I'm so glad you're here. Please, let me show you to your room."

After fussing over us for what felt like an eternity, the man closed the door behind him and left us alone. "Is it my imagination or was that a kelpie?" I asked, throwing myself backward onto the bed and linking my arms behind my neck. One thing these old palaces had in common was the beautiful ceiling work. Modern life had us all staring at plain white paint, but the people of yore added interest and art even to their ceilings. "Isn't he a little far from home?"

Fouchard lifted the suitcase to the top of the wood luggage rack and opened it. "Humans immigrate too, don't they?"

I snorted, my eyes happily roaming over the intricate woodwork of the ceiling. "Why are you asking me that? I'm not a human, remember?" I was joking, but there was still a touch of bitterness in those words. To find out I was a magical after a lifetime of thinking I was just an odd duckling was hard to get used to.

My merrow stopped what he was doing and came around the wide, white linen-covered bed and leaned over my face, his handsome dark features triggering a stampede inside my chest. "You're half human, idiot," he said with his usual finesse. "Druids are humans, you know?"

Like a kid, I snorted again. "A human with powerful magic is a magical, my sweet but deluded merrow." I doubted other humans would agree with my father's classification as a mere Homo sapiens.

Fouchard leaned further and kissed my mouth briefly. Fire erupted and quickly spread to every inch of my body, with special emphasis in one particular extremity. Before he could straighten, I wrapped a hand around his neck and pulled him over me. My boyfriend was a giant of a man, but the weight of his sexy body crushing mine felt like a caress.

He laughed. "Don't you want to start asking questions?" My freaking investigation could wait. This throbbing urgency in my pants couldn't.

It was pitch-dark outside by the time we emerged from our room, looking for food like two foraging bears awake from hibernation. The restaurant was still open but the food sounded too frou-frou for both our tastes, so we walked across the way to a small restaurant we had eaten in before and satisfied our hunger with pasta and simple but delicious seafood dishes. It was only then, with my belly full and my most basic instincts satisfied, that I felt ready to question some of the hotel staff. Rumor had it that the stolen tail had been in the possession of its owner, a certain Mr. Samaki, during his stay at the hotel.

"Did anything out of the ordinary happen while Mr. Samaki was here?" I asked the receptionist, the same giraffe dude who had greeted us on arrival.

He bit his lip before answering. "Well, he did invite a group of people to come and see the tail. He even reserved our conference room for it." He tapped two fingers on his chin. "There were ten or fifteen people here."

"Anyone caught your eye? Maybe acting suspicious or something?" I was grasping at straws, but there were no stupid questions when it came to investigating a crime. You'd be surprised with what people often notice without realizing it.

Giraffe-guy gave it another moment of thought. "There was a woman who seemed to be too interested in the layout of the hotel," he finally said. "She kept asking about exits and staffing and how long the tail would be on display."

My ears perked up. "Do you have her name?"

He shook his head and I deflated. "But she told me she owns a specialty store in Lisbon." I snapped my head up all ears and waited while he squinted. "What was it called?" He tapped his long fingers on his forehead now and squinted some more. He looked as if he was in pain. Suddenly he lifted his index finger up to the sky. "Yes, I remember. It was *Sereia do Tejo*, some New-Age-type store in downtown Lisbon."

Fouchard took out his phone and googled the name of the store. "Here it is," he said, showing me the search results. "Rua de S. Julião." He lowered his voice. "*Sereia do Tejo* means Tagus Mermaid." I should have known that, but even though my Portuguese was a thousand times better than when I first met my merman, it was still pretty rudimentary. Apparently, language was not a forte of mine, unlike magic.

"That sounds pretty promising," I mumbled. "Thank you for your help." I had already begun to walk away when I thought of something else. "Excuse me, Mr...." I let it hang awkwardly. Couldn't remember the kelpie's name. "Could you put us down for breakfast in bed tomorrow?"

The tall man nodded and scribbled something on his tablet. Fouchard bent down and whispered, "Breakfast in bed? Why? The restaurant is in the building."

I was so hoping he would ask. With the wickedest smile I could muster, I said, "Trust me, after what I have planned for you tonight, you're not going to want to get out of bed."

I could have easily stayed in that bed all day, cuddled tightly against my man, running my ever-hungry hands over his fabulous bod and conjuring images of erotic and nearly acrobatic things we could try later. But alas! We had to check out of the hotel by noon, so we dragged ourselves out of our love nest, took a shower in the ridiculously tiny bathtub—well, perfectly sized for one person but we were two big guys—got dressed, and left after munching on the delicious in-room breakfast. We didn't go far. In fact, we kept the car parked by the hotel and wandered into town on foot.

The hotel was built right on the eastern fringe of

Paço de Arcos, a small town on what the locals called *Linha de Cascais*, which roughly translated to Cascais Line. It stood, just as Carcavelos and Cascais, in a line of sandy beaches stretching westward from Lisbon to where the river Tagus met the Atlantic Ocean. There was a good bakery at a corner in the main road and several great coffee shops. Uphill from the church and not too far from the train station, there was a great *churrasqueira*, a delivery restaurant specializing in the ever-popular Portuguese open-flame grilled chicken.

"We should order some *churrasco* to go," I suggested, as my mind made its rounds of food-related places in the area.

Fouchard laughed and slid his hand in mine. "You only have two things in your mind: food and sex."

"And what's wrong with that?" I replied with a snort. "Maybe we should try both at the same time," I suggested, a crooked smile on my lips.

"Think again, my love," my merman said. "Despite popular belief, those two things should be kept separate. Trust me."

I stopped suddenly, our arms stretching between us as he kept walking for a few feet. "Wait! Are you talking from experience?" The sting of jealousy left a hole in my gut.

Naël turned to me and grimaced. "Maybe." He

didn't sound so sure now. The green-eyed monster must have been pretty obvious on my face. He waved a hand in the air dismissively. "It was a long time ago, sweetheart, when I was still young and stupid."

"You're not getting away that easy," I growled and hated myself immediately. I knew my man had lovers before me. Gods knew I had lost count of how many *I* had, but knowing and hearing him talk about it were two very different things. "Who did you try this food sex with and why?"

He shook his head and held me by my shoulders. "Stop the jealousy," he said. "I was in college, went to a party, got seriously drunk and decided it would be a great idea to bring food and a lover to bed at the same time." I tried to walk away but he held me still. "It wasn't. Neither the food nor the lover. I can't remember his name—or his face—and ended up with a terrible allergic rash in spots I prefer not to mention. Are you going to tell me you've never done something stupid like that?"

Despite myself I had to laugh. "Was it painful?" I managed to say, anger and jealousy gone.

He shook his head again and dropped his chin. "You have no idea. I walked bowlegged for days after."

A bark of laughter escaped me and Naël joined in.

"The fierce cranky merman gets beaten by a vegetable," I said.

We resumed our walking. "It was fruit actually," he added between laughs. "I do not recommend it."

We walked in the park, in and out of stores, and bought some warm bread before jumping in the car and driving back home.

I was quiet for a long while, watching the ocean as we drove on the *Marginal*, the road that snaked along the coast all the way to Cascais, and half listening to Christmas music on the radio.

"Are you okay?" Naël finally asked. "You're unusually quiet."

I looked at him then, relishing the smoothness of his brown skin, the way the corner of his eyes crinkled as he squinted against the winter sunshine, the fullness of his lips. "I was just thinking," I said. "It might work if we take antihistamines beforehand."

For a fraction of a second, Fouchard took his eyes off the road and the car veered dangerously to the other lane. "Are you fucking crazy?"

"Crazy for you, my sexy merrow," I said with a wink. "And okay, crazy period."

Fouchard shook his head with a chuckle. "You're lucky I love you so much, Aiden."

"I love you too, sweetheart," I replied. "We could try a carrot. You know, vitamin A and all that...."

The look my man gave me could melt an iceberg in seconds. "No. Food. Period. Got it?"

All right. A discussion for another time then.

CHAPTER 5

All I Want for Christmas is a Merman Tail

I ducked again, but my short brown hair still got caught by the many chimes hanging from the ceiling of the small downtown shop. I tried to disentangle myself from them, but all I managed was to make it worse.

"Fuck these things. They're noisy and dangerous." I looked like a fish caught on a net. It was humiliating.

"Oh, shut up, Aiden. You're such a baby." Taz rushed to my rescue, her high heels tapping on the tiled floor. How come the freaking chimes were not snagging on her wide-brimmed hat? Was the witch using her magic? She looked around her and then wiggled her fingers to free me from the evil items. "If you weren't so tall it wouldn't be a problem."

"Isn't it a bit biased to decorate a store thinking

only of short people?" I was a couple inches over six feet but hardly a giant. Maybe compared to the shrimpy store owner who couldn't be an inch more than five feet tall. "You're tall and wearing that sombrero, how come you're not getting ensnared by these damned things?"

She wiggled her fingers up in the air again. *Right, magic!*

Finally free, I closed in on the counter, my eyes straying over the packed shelves that covered the walls of the narrow rectangular shop. Vee would love the vast selection of everything unicorn, dragon, and mermaid, from soaps to clothing items. *Wait! Is that a jockstrap?* I shook my head in disbelief and flattened my hands on the wooden counter.

"Miss," I called. The short, brown-haired clerk, who I assumed was the owner, turned around to face me. There was nothing extraordinary about her—not a magical—and yet she had that kind of face that always feels familiar. "I'm working with the local police investigating a theft and I need to ask you some questions, if that's okay with you." Even if it wasn't, I would still ask them anyway.

"Investigation?" Her squeaky voice didn't match her rather somber face. "I'll help however I can." Why could all these people speak English so well when I was having so much trouble learning the local language?

"I understand you attended an exhibition of a silicone mertail at the Palácio dos Arcos hotel a week or so ago," I started, still a bit dazed by the profusion of tacky items surrounding me. She nodded. "The tail went missing afterward and you asked a lot of questions about the setting for the exhibition—"

"Are you insinuating I had something to do with it?" she interrupted me, crossing her arms over her chest.

It wasn't easy to fluster me. "Well, it *is* a bit suspicious that you'd be asking about emergency exits and things like that."

"For your information, I was asking all those questions because I was hoping to hold a merpeople conference at the hotel." Wait, she knew about merfolk?

Taz was at my side. "The merpeople community spans several continents, Aiden," she said with a tiny smile. Then she whispered, hiding her words from the clerk with her hat. "They're regulars who dress like merfolk, not real merpeople." There were so many things I still didn't know, even in my late thirties.

The little woman continued, "Also I was very interested in finding out where Mr. Samaki had purchased his tail. Mine is getting old and I need a new one, but my silicone tailor has retired." *There is such a thing as silicone tailors?*

I cleared my throat. "If that's the case, maybe you can remember something unusual or suspicious." I know I was fishing on mostly dry land but I wasn't giving up that easy. "A conversation, a look, anything at all."

"I don't know whether this means anything, but yesterday I was in a forum on MerNetwork and there was a guy who kept saying he had a brand new, one-of-a-kind tail he wanted to sell for an incredibly high price." *There are merpeople forums?* "It's not weird that he was trying to sell the tail—lots of people sell things through the forum—but it was the fact he refused to show a picture of the tail. How did he expect people to pay an excess of 3,000 euros for something they hadn't even seen yet?"

She was right about that; it was pretty suspicious. "Do you remember the name of the seller?" Taz was inspecting a particularly nefarious-looking Neptune figurine, her perfectly shaped eyebrows knitted together.

"We all use an alias in the forum and he was not a registered merchant, but he identified himself as MurúchFir from the Euro Pod." *Gaelic? I'm not sure how I knew that, but I did. Maybe it was the druid* blood running in my veins. "I can give you the URL to the forum if you'd like." Not sure what help that would be, I nodded and watched her as she scribbled something on a mermaid-shaped notepad.

Vee would get along famously with this wannabe mermaid.

Besides the fact Fouchard was hot as lava and the mere thought of him made my pants shrink, there were other advantages to dating a merrow: one, you could, unlike other normal humans, stay underwater for a significant amount of time with the help of his magic breath, and two, he had contacts no one else had, including Neptune and a gaggle of pretty young mermaids who couldn't stop swooning over his well-toned body.

"Mary said to call her this morning," Fouchard said, taking a giant bite of an apple. We had eaten breakfast around the marble-top kitchen island and were still perching on the high stools while Vee continued to stuff her mouth with french toast. The girl could eat her weight in food. "She knows one of the local admins to MerNetwork. He can maybe help you find out who this MurúchFir is."

I could only hope. Things got a bit murky once it came to online sites. All the new European regulations made finding things online almost impossible at times. Where was a talented hacker when you needed one?

"Taz said she might have found the perfect venue for your wedding," Vee announced, her cheeks dilated and puffy like a squirrel, bits of bread flying out of her mouth.

I handed her a napkin. "Don't spray it, girl. I forgot my umbrella." She made a face at me and opened her mouth wide so I could have a better—and totally undesired—look inside. I pretend-gagged.

Fouchard tsked, shaking his head. "Damn, Aiden, sometimes I wonder if I'm getting a husband or another little sibling."

I threw him a killer stare. "So where exactly is this amazing venue, Vee?"

The white-haired imp had resumed her french toast attack, stuffing as much as she could into her small mouth. She chewed in silence for a moment and then grumbled, "Some place in Sintra."

Not Sintra again! It was such a beautiful, magical place—emphasis on the magical—but that was part of the problem; it wasn't as if I wanted to keep magic out of my wedding, because let's face it, I couldn't even if I did. It was that the green hills of Sintra, with its exquisite architecture and unique native species, held too many bad memories—memories that always seemed to eclipse the good ones.

Vee swallowed whatever she had left in her mouth. "She said to call her later and she'd tell you about it." Knowing Taz, chances were she'd show up when least expected.

There was a knock on the door and Vee sprung off the stool in a perfect imitation of a Jack-in-the-Box and ran to open it. "It's Cristina," she yelled.

I glanced at Fouchard who was drinking his fourth cup of coffee. He claimed coffee didn't affect merfolk. Doubtful.

"Cristina and Silva are taking her to the movies," my merrow clarified.

It was barely eleven in the morning. What kind of movie were they watching? "This early?"

"Shopping first." Fouchard took another sip before sliding to his feet. "Apparently there is a new novelty shop in the mall. Lots of unicorns and rainbows." His chuckle pulled at the corners of my lips. That man could always make me smile.

Vee came back, tugging an overly tolerant Cristina. My best friend smiled as soon as she saw me. It still made my heart bleed to see the scars in her face, scars that I was to blame for. Yes, Bob, the Idiot God, had done it, but I had been the one stirring up his anger.

"Wait! Who's watching the store?" Deflecting was my not-so-hidden talent. I knew exactly who was—or was not—watching my coffee shop, Bicas R Us. I had decided we all needed a break and some "family time," so I closed the place for one Sunday. Vee could get her fix of hanging out with my best friend and only employee, and I could get extra freaky with my merman.

Cristina rolled her eyes. Behind her, the stunning warlock cop who she was unwisely engaged to waved at us before stuffing his hands in the pockets of his jeans. It seemed as if he also had a day off.

"We're going to go shopping for unicorn stuff, then lunch at the Time Out Market, go look at the ducks at Duck Store, and then watch the movie, *Mermaids*." I was out of breath just listening to her. God, Cristina was truly a saint. And Silva? Was he really that patient with kids too or was he just putting on a show to charm my friend? Maybe he'd make a good father after all.

"You do know that movie is not really about mermaids, right?" I said, party-pooper that I was.

The little imp stuck her tongue out at me. "I know, but it's about accepting who you are," she said, the wisdom of a much older woman coming through. "You probably should watch it yourself, Aiden, since you are still struggling with accepting your magical background." Sometimes that child was too smart.

"All right, little Miss Muffet, I got it," I said, shooing her toward the door. "Go have fun with my best friend. I will try my best not to get bored with your old brother."

Cristina laughed and ushered her toward the door, hands on her shoulders. "Let's go and leave the old people alone. I'm sure they can come up with something to entertain themselves." Cristina's lips quirked up as she winked at me. "We, the young and wild, are going to have fun. Let's go."

Nobody pointed out that Vee was still wearing her breakfast, bits of toast clinging to the sides of her mouth and her shirt. Silva would most likely magic her back into tidiness as soon as they were out the door. A wave of his long fingers and poof! All clean.

As soon as the door closed behind them, I turned around to face my merman. "Whatever shall we do now?" I hoped my one-sided smile would be enough of a hint of what I had in mind.

Fouchard didn't disappoint. "Now that I ate all this bread, I'm very hungry for something else." Pantshrinking alert! "Shall we finish breakfast in our room?"

My inner furnace was blazing, and if I didn't get rid of my jeans soon, they'd explode. "Better yet, let's take it into the shower, shall we?"

By the time we crashed through the bedroom door, entangled in each other, I had already lost my shoes and pants, and my shirt was hanging by a thread. This was going to be an amazing breakfast.

CHAPTER 6

O Christmas Aiden

They say that when you have a sore spot somewhere in your body, you are sure to constantly hit it again. As if pain attracts more pain. Sintra was my sore spot, and yet, here I was again, walking through the streets of the beautiful town.

"Is it really possible that there are no other wedding venues in Lisbon or the suburbs?" I whined, not for the first time. Since this place in particular was not quite in the old town, we had stopped on the way at the Casa do Preto, a small coffee shop on the outskirts where we fed on *queixadas* and drowned in good espresso. I would be on a sugar high for a few hours.

Predictably, Taz rolled her eyes as she wiped her mouth on a napkin. "Stop the bellyaching already. I think you will love this place. It's not far from the Palácio dos Seteais." I grumbled and took my last bite of the sweet cheese pastry. "And quit the bear noises. You are such a baby."

I grumbled a bit more, wiped my mouth, and got on my feet. "Let's get this over with. I'm starting to break out in hives." Not really, but I had a flair for the melodramatic.

We drove the remaining few miles to the site, a nondescript small house with whitewashed walls nestled in the woods with a big, round, colorful sign depicting a Franciscan monk with a beer in his hand. Little did these people know that an order of very unusual monks lived just up the road from them. There was a smallish, wooden sign hanging to the side of the front door that read, Pub Medieval—which I gathered must mean Medieval Pub; even I could figure that one out—and a disturbing stone sculpture of a faun over the doorway.

I threw Taz an incredulous glance. "Really? Another magical site?" I growled.

"Don't get your panties all in a twist, Aiden," she said, stepping in front of me and walking inside. "There is nothing magical about this place. It's called

Casa do Fauno, idiot. Faun's House is just a wonderful medieval-inspired place to eat and drink with friends."

Still skeptic, I followed her inside. It was dark, the maroon and yellow walls washed by the faint light coming through a big window. Wooden trestle tables and benches filled the inside with a large hearth and a brightly decorated Christmas tree as the focus of the main wall. It was a cozy place where I could see myself and my merman lounging for an afternoon or an evening of fado and beer, but for a wedding?

"Don't knock it just yet, my doubting friend," Taz said, leading me to the back of the restaurant. "You haven't seen the best part."

Sure enough, as we emerged from the building into the backyard, I gasped. There was a whole large courtyard, shaded by trees and framed by bushes and rows of what I was certain would be flowers in the spring. Small tables and chairs were scattered along the sides and against the wall of the house where the white was broken by a large blue and white tile picture. It was beautiful and magical, without the actual magic.

I liked it.

"You're smiling," Taz exclaimed as if I couldn't tell myself. "That must mean you are considering it. And you thought I couldn't find you a great venue."

"Wipe that smug smile from your face, witch," I

snapped, not quite able to not smile myself. The little witch had done well. "The place is... suitable."

"Idiot," she growled, plopping herself on one of the chairs and waving a server over. "Bring us a *Poção da Bruxa* and a *Bafo de Dragão* and some goat cheese." The flustered server walked away and Taz crossed her legs, pouting.

"What did you just order?" I asked her, sitting across from her. It was cold and we were the only fools sitting outside.

"Witch's Brew and Dragon Breath, two of their specialty meads." Whatever had been eating her a second before was gone. One of the things I liked about her: slow to anger and quick to forgive. "They're really good."

"You're not going to get drunk again, are you?" I said, recalling our last adventure together. "The goats were cute but they stank."

She humphed. "That was not my fault. The monks' brew has something in it that doesn't agree with me."

"Yeah, alcohol," I added, not helpfully at all.

The server brought two ceramic mugs of a honey-scented drink and left just as quickly, throwing strange looks at the witch who was now wearing her gigantic hat and sunglasses—two things she did not have on her on arrival.

"Shall we reserve the place for your wedding?" she asked after taking a long sip of the drink.

I sniffed the mug, a little suspicious of its contents. "Not sure yet, Taz," I said. "I do like it a lot, but it's so far from the ocean. Naël wants to invite Neptune, and the old man doesn't like to wander too far from the coast. Besides, I want my groom to be in a place that makes him feel alive, and for a merman, only the ocean can do that."

"You just want him to be good and ready to get kinky after the ceremony." Well, there was that, but for once I really meant it; I wanted the wedding venue to be one Naël would feel at home in. He'd love this place, but something was still not right.

"I'll add it to the list of possible venues."

"How long is that list?" Taz asked, taking another sip.

"As of right now, it's a list of one." I sighed.

I was so freaking screwed.

The little slave master, also known as Vee, bit her lower lip and rubbed her chin as if deciding how to further torture me. After all, for Vee, bullying the adults was a science. I couldn't help it; my inner teenager came out. I rolled my eyes and whined, "Will you get on with it already? I have a business to run, little mermaid."

Vee's disapproving gaze fell on me with surprising impact. I actually shivered. "Patience is a virtue, Aiden," she said deadpan, giving me another once-over. I must have looked ridiculous with tinsel hanging from my ears, Christmas garland wrapped around my neck like a scarf, and big red baubles pinned to my T-shirt and hanging from my fingers. "Something is missing." *Yes, my dignity.* If someone walked into the living room at that time and saw me in that getup, I may have to commit hara-kiri to save face.

The little imp had managed to enlist my help in planning how to decorate the Christmas tree. Of course, at the time I thought she meant she needed me to help her hang trinkets on the enormous evergreen tree my merman had brought home with him the day before. Little did I know she meant she'd use my body as the drafting canvas.

"Come on, Vee, I'm starting to itch and I can't even scratch because I have baubles tied to my digits." I was not above begging a twelve-year-old for mercy. She was a master at using my guilt about the lack of unicorns or fake mermaid decorations at my wedding. Of course, we were still missing a venue as well, so it was kind of a moot point. "Why not try this on the actual tree. Vee? I'm not green or tall enough."

She humphed and stomped the few feet between us to start unraveling the shiny, bright objects she was tormenting me with. "If you didn't want to help me, you should have said so in the first place," she growled, her lower lip stuck so far out I could probably hang a bauble there. "Naël is too busy, you're too whiny, Taz is working at her parlor today, and you work Cristina like a slave. So, who's going to help me?" The child used guilt with the finesse of a skilled swordsman.

I cupped the back of her neck with a bedazzled hand and pulled her in for a hug. "I want to help you, silly, but I'd prefer if I'm not used as a Christmas tree," I said with a chuckle. "All this tinsel is giving me hives."

She giggled a little against my chest and then pulled away, her hair snagging on the trinkets attached to my hands. "Okay, let me get it all out."

After a few tense moments trying to undo the cruel, however festive decorations on my humiliated self, I made us some hot cocoa, and together we began decorating the real tree. Naël had some vintage trea-sures in his storage boxes, beautiful figurines of merfolk with glittering tails and sparkling hair. They looked custom-made.

"They belonged to my parents," Vee said as if she'd heard my unspoken question. I froze with a gorgeously delicate figurine of a merman angel dangling from my fingers. "Naël says they used to have a famous merartist create a new one every year."

I moved my gaze from the little imp to the ornament. It was exquisite in its detail. Each tiny scale on its glittering white tail seemed unique, and the feathers of its wings rivaled the real thing. "Beautiful," I murmured, fangirling slightly.

"Naël told me the sculptor is known as the Michelangelo of merfolk," Vee added, over-enunciating the artist's name. I chuckled and resumed our decorating.

Once the little sour patch kid quit decorating me, the afternoon rolled by quickly and pleasantly. I realized with a jolt that I had never decorated a tree, much less with a family member. Christmas Eve had always been a lonely affair for me, with a mini pre-decorated tree in a corner of the house and a naked man in my bed. Christmas morning was even lonelier, as said naked man rushed out to be with his family and friends. This—this hanging out with my soon-to-be sister-in-law, trimming a huge tree, drinking hot cocoa and eating sparkly cookies—was heartwarming and just plain nice. For the hundredth time, I was stricken with the knowledge that I now had a family too.

"Now, that's something you don't see every day." Naël was standing in the doorway, leaning against the doorframe with his arms crossed tightly. My man was beautiful. Both Vee and I looked up at him. "A mermaid and a demigod druid trimming a tree."

Vee ran to him and wrapped her skinny amber arms around his waist. "My brother is here to help us," she squealed in perfect imitation of a piglet. Fouchard looked at me with a one-sided smile and I shrugged, a stubborn grin fighting to come out. "You're the tallest, so we need you to put the mermaid-star on the top."

"Then you better let go of me or I will have to drag you across the room," Naël said, deadpan. The little mermaid let go of her brother and grinned, her perfect white teeth glittering in the growing shadows of the evening. My man rubbed his chin and squinted, studying the tree. "I gotta say, you guys did a good job. The tree looks amazing."

Like a little kid, my heart actually leapt inside my chest. "Really?" My lips tugged at the corners when my man smiled at me. "You really think so?" Gods, I did sound like a kid.

Fouchard let out a bark of a laugh and swooped

both me and his sister into a hug. "You guys are my life. Where would I be without you?"

I may have sniffled a little.

CHAPTER 7

Merman Wonderland

"**F**uck!" My language proficiency seemed to be on the decline. This was the fifth or sixth time I used the expletive in the last ten minutes.

Cristina, who was sitting on a chair across from me rubbing her first-trimester bump, looked up and frowned. "What now? Aiden, I thought Naël was the cranky one."

"This forum is harder to break into than Fort Knox," I whined, hitting my forehead on the laptop keyboard—very lightly. I was no masochist. "I have been looking for this MurúchFir for a couple days and I still haven't been able to find him. Everyone knows who he is but no one is talking. I feel I may have stumbled on something much more serious than a mertail-napping."

"I thought Mary was going to help you with that," Cristina said.

"Dead end," I grumbled, punching a few random keys on the laptop as if that would help. "Don't know what else to do."

She stood up and circled around the table to come and stand by me, peering at the screen. "Move over, red rover," she ordered, emphasizing her words with a not-so-gentle shove. "Let the experts do it."

I snorted. "You? An expert in merfolk forums?" It was preposterous, considering she was not even a magical. Oh wait! Neither were any of these so-called mers in the forum. "What makes you think you can find something I've been trying to track in vain for the past few days?"

She braced her hands on her hips and tilted her head in a perfect imitation of Vee. "I may not have magic, but no one beats me on social forums." That was news to me. I had seen her mess with her notebook many times, but I thought all she was doing was checking emails and Facebook messages.

Still a bit stunned by the revelation, I moved my chair to the side and she pulled another one by me. Her fingers started a frantic tip-tapping dance on the keyboard while her eyes followed every word on the screen. She held her lower lip between her teeth and scrolled through row after row of information, stopping here and there to comment with a question.

"How are you in the forum if you don't have an account?" I asked, feeling I had missed something important.

"When you told me about this a few days ago, I was curious, so I created my own account." I'll be damned. Why hadn't I thought of that? I was navigating the forum as a guest, which only gave me access to a limited number of places within the site. "If you ever feel the need to find me online, I am SereiaBela."

I couldn't help it; I snorted again. "Beautiful mermaid? Really? Can you be any more bigheaded?" Okay, so I was feeling a little spiteful for not having thought of doing the same myself. "You're not even one of them."

"Does it matter?" Of course it did. Would you join a medieval reenactment group if you didn't enjoy dressing up like a sixteenth century knight and playing with swords? Would you join a tea-lovers club if you didn't drink tea? "I have made a few new friends, and who knows, maybe come summer I'll buy a mertail and join them for some fun in the sun."

"It will have to be a pretty large size tail to accommodate your nine-month baby bump," I said. "That, I'll pay to see."

Her hand had not lost its power with the pregnancy hormones. She slapped me over the back of my head and my teeth actually rattled. "This child will be born in June, in plenty of time for me to lose all the weight and wear a bikini again." She raised her hands from the keyboard in a dramatic gesture. "There! Done. I have tracked him down and set up a meeting with him for tomorrow."

I did a double take. "What?" My gaze flew to the screen. "How did you do that?"

"I told him you were looking for a one-of-a-kind tail and willing to pay a fortune for it." My friend Cristina was a genius. I leaned over, bookended her cheeks with my hands, and planted a loud kiss on her forehead. "You owe me a box of *trouxas de ovos*," she added with a smile.

"What's this thing with the egg pastries lately?" She'd been constantly running or asking someone to run to the *pastelaria* across the square to get some of the sinful egg delicacies.

"Baby cravings." Doubtful. She had also been "craving" lobster, which Silva obediently picked up from a local restaurant every other day. I hoped that cops were better paid in Portugal than in the US or he would soon go bankrupt. My friend stood up, rubbing her belly again, and had stepped away a few feet before turning around and saying, "Oh yeah, I may have promised him a date also." I knitted my brow. "With you, *idiota*, not me."

Great. Months ago, this would have probably been an exciting prospective, but I was happily mated with a *real* merman now. "Thank you, Cristina," I yelled out as she walked away toward the *copa*. "It's always nice when friends look out for you."

If sarcasm were water, Cristina would have drowned.

Naël straightened my peacoat lapels again. "Will you stop squirming for a sec?" he barked, his lips set into a scowl that would scare the daylights out of anyone, except me. I knew there was a soft core to that tough facade. "It's not like you're actually on a real date. And since when did dating make you nervous?"

I grabbed one of his wrists and held it tight. "Since I committed to the crankiest of mermen, of course." I brought his hand to my lips and kissed his knuckles. "It makes me feel dirty, as if I'm cheating on you."

A tiny smile kicked one corner of his lips. "Are you

considering it?"

My brow furrowed so deeply it hurt. "Hell no. You know I left my promiscuous life behind me for good." He laughed softly. *Evil man!* "Stop teasing me. You know you are all I want and need, or I wouldn't be marrying you."

My hot merman chuckled again, one hand still on my lapel, and bent down slightly to place a kiss on my lips. "And you better not forget it, you handsome demigod you." He was the only one who could evoke my ancestry and make it sound as if it was a good thing.

I was about to meet with the forum merchant who was also quite possibly the thief we'd been looking for. Thanks to Cristina—good thing I loved her—I was also supposed to pretend this was some kind of weird blind date. I was not a happy camper.

Naël turned me around, patted my butt, and said, "Go, my love, go break this guy's heart and then come back to me."

I humphed and left. My fiancé had offered to drive me, but I'd rather walk. This fake merman was meeting me at a local coffee shop just ten minutes from Naël's house, and I could use that time to collect myself.

Just a job. Get him to admit where he got the tail and then leave. Easy-peasy.

Right, then why were my insides all in a tangle?

By the time I arrived at the coffee shop, I swear I must have been wearing my stomach inside out. I dashed to the counter to order a toast and a bica before sitting down at a free table inside. Cristina, evil woman that she was, had set it up so that I had to wear a ridiculous scarlet carnation on my lapel for the suspect to identify me as his "date." I looked like one of those red-light district pimps with the fake flower attached to my peacoat. I shivered.

"Are you SereiaBela?" a slimy voice asked me.

My gaze flew up and met with the strangest-looking man I had ever seen. His pasty complexion resembled rotten milk and he had a nearly flat nose—really, it couldn't even qualify as such. It was more like two small holes on his face. His light brown eyes tipped down on the outside edges, giving him a permanent sad expression despite the bright pupils. And his hair, oh, by all that was holy, was that even real hair? Strands of dirty blond hair hung from his head to his shoulders. I couldn't help but to feel sorry for this guy. I could only imagine how much teasing he had to put up with his whole life.

A magical after all. Not sure what kind. Possibly a mélange of different ones.

"Yes, and you are the Celtic merman." It was not a

question. I could see strange, flimsy flippers sticking out from his back. My one original power didn't let me down; I could still see through the veil of magical deception. "What are you really? You're not a full merman."

I couldn't be sure but I think he grimaced—hard to tell with a face like that. "I have merfolk ancestry," he countered, sounding not too pleased with my statement. Then, in a quieter voice, he added, "And water sprite." That explained the nose. "And *maruxinho*," he whispered.

Now, that *was* interesting. His ears, large and almost pointy, confirmed him as the Portuguese garden-variety elf. I had read about them but never actually seen one. Not that this one was a full-blood. He was a mess of mixed magical ancestry. I couldn't help feeling sorry for him; I knew exactly how that felt.

"Why are you part of a fake merfolk group then?" I asked, curious in spite of myself. The funny-looking dude sat down, his disproportionately long legs crossed at the ankles. "Isn't that kind of redundant?" I really wanted to say stupid, but I needed information and I supposed getting on his wrong side was probably not the way to achieve that.

"I cannot morph into a merman or a water sprite," he grunted rather than spoke. Obviously, a tender, sensitive subject for him. "My flippers and fins never developed enough and neither did my gills." He stretched his short neck forward with a slight twist, exposing the area closest to his Baby Yoda ears. Instead of gills he had something that looked a lot more like half-healed scratches. "So, this group allows me to do what my DNA does not."

It made a warped kind of sense. At least I had received the powers my parents had; he, on the other hand, had received only the bad characteristics—that hair in particular was obviously a mutation of some kind.

"Maybe we should get to business," I said, hoping to all gods that he had forgotten about the date part. "Do you still have that tail?"

The *maruxinho* leaned across the table and tried to hold one of my hands, but I was quicker and managed to pull it away before his sultana skin touched mine. I restrained a shiver at the disappointed expression on his face.

"I really, really liked that tail and am willing to pay a small fortune for it," I announced, trying not to look too repulsed.

He let out a long sigh. "How small?" Greedy little jackass.

"Not that small," I answered, wanting nothing else

than to race out of there and away from that creepy guy. "Well, do you still have it?"

"I sold it a few days ago." What? Then why had he agreed to meet me? Did he actually think he could get in *my* pants? "But I have others equally beautiful. If you come with me to my place, I'll show you."

Yep, he did have elf in him after all. No, thank you. "I'm only interested in that one tail," I said, biting back some other well-deserved but most likely unwise words. "Who bought it? I'm willing to pay for the information."

His narrow shoulders slumped forward. "Some guy from a movie company." His eyes brightened up. "I have the address at home." *Hell, no, I won't go!* "Maybe after a nice dinner...."

The guy was obviously delusional. I leaned forward. "Listen, Mister, I need that name now." My detective voice was still there after all. "I am not going to your place and we will not cavort in any shape or form now or ever. But I can promise you a few days of pain if you refuse to give me this information." His eyes narrowed. The asshole didn't believe me. "If you want confirmation of how easily I can put you in a whole lot of pain, you can call the Warlock of Lisbon, Antonio Silva. He will tell you about my status as a demigod."

His jaw almost hit the table. I'm certain I saw beads of sweat dripping down his forehead onto his nose. "You're Aiden Mercer?"

I nodded, not sure whether to be happy my reputation preceded me. "Who is this person who bought the *stolen* tail from you?" I emphasized the word stolen just in case he needed further motivation to tell me the truth. I could have his butt in prison with a simple call to the warlock cop.

The *maruxinho* gulped. "Some guy working for the Cinemate studio." I lifted my butt halfway from the chair and he cringed. "Luis," he yelped. "Luis Andrade."

A slow, satisfied smile stretched across my lips. I stood up. "Good man," I whispered, pushing the chair in and digging inside my pants pocket for a couple bills. I placed them on the table. "This is for your trouble. Good luck." *You'll need it.*

The sooner I put some distance between us, the better. That dude seriously creeped me out. I punched in the emergency number on my cell—and no, not 1-1-2 but my merman's number—and waited for Naël to pick up while I dashed down the hill as if being pursued by a gang of vampires.

"Is everything okay?" Aww, my sweetie was

worried. It made my insides melt. "Where are you? I'll come and get you."

I shook my head. "No, sweetheart, no need," I said, picking up my pace. "I'm on my way home. I just had an urgent need to hear your voice."

A soft chuckle crossed the airwaves into my ears. "Do I sing to you or say something dirty?"

"I was thinking of sweet nothings, but dirty sounds good too," I said with a giant smile. "What are you wearing?"

I heard nothing but rustling sounds for a few moments. "I'm butt naked now," he finally said, his sexy voice low and full of promise. "Don't you have a handy-dandy teleporting gift? What are you waiting for? This bed is lonely without you in it."

He didn't have to ask twice. I closed my eyes, visualized our bed, and the next thing I knew I was getting an eyeful of my hot merrow. He was sprawling in bed, naked as promised, with tinsel around his neck like a scarf and a certain part of his manly anatomy stuffed inside a Christmas stocking.

"Christmas is almost here," he stated with a wicked smile and a wink. "I thought you may want to unwrap a gift ahead of time."

Ho-ho-ho! Merry Christmas to all and to me a good night.

CHAPTER 8

Frosty the Mertailnapper

Nothing made sense. Not the case I was working on and not my frantic search for a wedding venue. The wedding was less than two weeks away and I still hadn't been able to find the perfect spot.

"That's the problem," my pregnant friend said, taking another giant bite off a sandwich. "You want it to be perfect and there isn't such a thing."

I knew she was right but didn't care to admit it. "Where is all that food going anyway?" Deflect, I always say.

Cristina made a face. "This baby is a hungry little thing," she said, bits of crumbs flying out of her mouth. "Now that the morning sickness is done, it's almost as if she's making up for lost time."

"You seem pretty certain it's a girl," I said with a snort. "I will be laughing if you end up with a boy."

"It's a girl," she insisted. "Tó is sure." And was the warlock clairvoyant or something? How did he know? "And Taz had a vision." Shit. So maybe it *was* a girl after all. "But you're avoiding the subject. You need a venue for your wedding. Now."

I could feel a headache coming. I sighed. "I'll talk to Naël today and make a decision. In the meantime, I have to go to the Cinemate studio looking for an elusive tailnapper."

"Why don't you reach out to Oisin?" What could the Irish god have anything to do with movie production companies? "He has connections in the entertainment world." Of course he did. "He's made guest appearances in many Portuguese TV shows."

"Are you telling me Taz's red-haired main squeeze is a star?"

"I wouldn't say a star, but he has had screen time and knows a lot of people in the industry," Cristina said, standing up and swiping a tray from the counter. "Now I must attend to our customers." Not that there were many this early in the day. It was cold outside, a lot colder than the Portuguese were accustomed to, so most were still holed up in their homes waiting for the sun to warm up the air a bit before venturing out.

I watched her waltz to a table where an old man had just sat down, newspaper in hand. Maybe I would call on Oisin. I didn't know him very well, but he had been a great help during our final battle with Bob, the Idiot, and his mother. Besides he was Taz's boyfriend, so he couldn't be that bad. The witch was a little quirky and annoying but was an excellent judge of character. After all, she had trusted me from the get-go, hadn't she?

I pulled out my cell and searched for Oisin's number. The phone rang for a couple minutes before a sleepy voice picked up. "*I dtigh diabhail*, Aiden!"

"What did you just say?" Irish Gaelic was a hard language. I seemed to know a few words here and there, not sure why but possibly due to my druid DNA.

"Damn it, Aiden, I was asleep."

I looked at the clock on the wall, an eyebrow raised. "It's ten o'clock, oh mighty god. What were you doing last night? Cavorting with the witch again?"

He actually growled, and I had to laugh. Oisin was normally a very mild-mannered, calm dude, so to hear him this disgruntled from lack of sleep was hilarious. I filed that information for a later date when I might need something to tease him about.

"That's none of your business, Aiden." Which

meant a resounding yes. They were like two rabbits in heat—not that rabbits were ever not in heat. "What do you want?"

"Such a grumpy little god," I quipped, delighted to have pissed him off. Yes, I was a kid inside. "I understand you know people in the movie industry. I was wondering whether you could facilitate a meeting with someone."

"I don't do star-stalking." As if I would ever want to stalk anyone. Unless of course it was Jason Momoa or maybe even Ryan Reynolds.

"No stars," I assured him, my mind now full of images of Momoa's tattoos. "Just a crew member who may have stolen a precious, fake merman tail."

The sound got muffled for a moment but my freakish hearing clearly heard Taz asking him if he wanted a cup of coffee. "Make it a double, witch," I yelled out.

"He has superman hearing." Taz's voice came through loud and clear. "No point in hiding it from him. Yes, Mercer, I'm here."

I chuckled. "You must have not been too good last night for him to be this cranky." Hit them where it hurts.

"I was too good, my friend." Was there no way to annoy this woman? "I made him work too hard." She giggled like a twelve-year-old. "I'll bring you some coffee, Oisin."

Silence filled the airwaves for a moment. "Who exactly do you need to talk to anyway?"

"Someone called Luis Andrade, not sure what his job is." Or care, really. I just wanted to talk to him and get this mystery out of the way before my wedding.

"Thank you, Taz." A gurgling sound followed before he answered me. "I know him. Be ready tomorrow at noon and I will take you to him."

I couldn't believe my luck. Every piece of this puzzle seemed to fall in place a bit too easily. I was beginning to be very suspicious.

"Something is very fishy indeed," I muttered to myself.

"I've told you before; merrows are not related to fish." My sweet and hot merman was standing behind me looking good enough to eat. "And I definitely do not smell fishy."

I stood up and turned to him with that foolish smile he always brought out of me. "I was talking about this case, not you, my sexy lover." I wrapped my arms around his waist and drew him close. "But I would love you even if you smelled like a fish."

He dropped a kiss on my lips and squeezed me tighter. "Fool. I'm not a tuna."

We sat down, side by side, our knees touching. "Naël, I'm beginning to think it was a terrible idea to put me in charge of finding a wedding venue," I told him, my elbows resting on my knees. "I can't find anything remotely good or that won't bring any of us bad memories."

He leaned over and covered my hands with his. "Sweetheart, no worries," he whispered, his amazing dark eyes searching for mine. "I have found the perfect place."

I opened my eyes wide. "What? You did?"

Fouchard laughed and kissed me again, this time longer. "Yes, it was under our noses—figuratively and literally—all this time." I raised my eyebrows. "We will get married in the one spot we both feel most at home." I tilted my head like a bird. He snorted. "You don't seem very confident that I, the best merman in your life, could come up with the perfect solution to our wedding woes."

I covered his mouth with mine and kissed him long and deeply, my tongue showing him—I hoped—how much I believed in him. We were both breathless by the time we pulled away. "Go on. Where's this place?"

His delicious lips twisted to one side in a lopsided smile. "Our underground beach."

Fuck! Why hadn't I thought about that?

Perfect, that would be absolutely perfect.

It was as if someone had removed the fifty-ton boulder I'd been carrying on my shoulders for the past few weeks. Knowing we had the perfect location for our wedding had cleared my mind and allowed me to focus on other pressing matters like what I would wear and what kind of cake to order—I voted for a giant donut while my mate was leaning toward something a bit more traditional. Also, it gave me time and energy to come up with excuses not to add anything unicorn to our wedding bliss. It was easier said than done. Vee could be a very determined little mermaid.

"Are you still heading out with Oisin today?" Naël asked me from the bathroom. I leaned over sideways a bit to try and take a gander at my naked mate, but the door was half closed. I sighed, frustrated. "I thought you had planned for yesterday."

I slid my feet into the boots and wriggled my toes. Gods, I couldn't wait for summer and to be able to wear my beloved flip-flops again. "We had, but Bicas R Us was too busy yesterday and I couldn't leave Cristina to fend for herself," I said, staring woefully at my comfortable slippers as my toes moaned inside the winter footwear. "So, we rescheduled for today. Do you want to come?"

My merrow came out of the bathroom—sadly already fully dressed—drying his hair with a towel. "I can't," he said. "I promised Vee I would bring a cake for her class Christmas party. Today is the last day of school before the break."

Drama queen that I was, I sighed deeply. "Your little sister sure knows how to ruin my day." Not true. I loved her to death and was more than happy to share my lover's attention with her.

"The only celebrity I care for is the druid god who shares my bed."

Aw, he could be so sweet sometimes.

I swallowed him, my tongue seeking his. It didn't have to look far; he met each of my strokes with one of his own, and in ten seconds flat, I was hard as a rock.

"Damn, now I need a cold shower," I said once we pulled away from each other. He laughed, the wicked man. "You think it's funny? Don't want to rain on your parade, but are you really going to go to Vee's school with a hard-on like that?" I pointed at his crotch. The stretched-out fabric of his pants left very little to the imagination.

"Fuck, Aiden," he exclaimed, half groaning, half

laughing. "We don't have time for this. I told the baker I'd pick up the cake in half an hour."

I offered him a lopsided smile. "I can be very quick," I suggested with another glance at his pants.

He shook his head and stepped away from me so fast you'd think I was on fire—which I was, but it was a very different kind of flame. "No way, sweetheart. You know my sister; she'll kill me if I am even one minute late. Gotta go." He looked down at his own tented pants and added, "Behave."

My laughter followed him out the door and I'm certain down the stairs. "You'll regret it!" I yelled out.

"Goodbye, my love," he yelled back from downstairs. The sound of the front door opening and closing announced his departure.

I was left with a vexing question and decision to make: did I jump in the shower and take care of this hard problem myself or did I try to ignore it and go meet the Irish god? You know what they say; if you want things done right, do it yourself. So, I did.

Some time later I arrived at Taz's apartment building where Oisin had been living ever since the Great Battle of the Idiot God—not an official title, just what I decided I'd call it; I was hoping it would stick and be in the history books of the future. One could dream.

"You're late." Taz didn't mince words. She had her arms crossed under her bosom, making her boobs look even more generous than they were already. "You made Oisin wait."

I bowed deeply, sarcasm dripping from my body language. "I apologize to the great god, Oisin, and beg for forgiveness," I said in what I hoped was a grave voice. "I had some pressing matters to take care of." Not a lie exactly.

The aforementioned god appeared beside the witch, a boyish smile on his face. "Don't mind her, Aiden," he said, draping an arm over Taz's shoulders. "We found something to do while we waited." *Geez, too much information.* I shivered in disgust as he planted a sloppy kiss on her cheek. "Come on in for a sec. Want a coffee?"

One never says no to a good cup of coffee. That's the golden rule in every coffee-lover's bible. By the time we left, we were already late to our appointment by at least an hour and a half. Good thing the Portuguese are pretty flexible with schedules. Surprisingly, Oisin waltzed through security with no problem whatsoever. Everyone seemed to know him and either treat him with some deference or as if they had been friends for years. After many claps on the back, high fives, and even a few fist bumps, we finally arrived at a small building that screamed administrative offices.

"He works here," the Irish god said, turning the doorknob and entering without knocking. Was he really that familiar with this place? Color me flabbergasted. The young god—if by young you mean a few hundred years—had Hollywood potential.

A young woman sat at a desk in the lobby, her pretty brown eyes focused on the computer screen in front of her. She lifted her head and offered us a formal smile at first, and then her whole face opened into a grin.

"Oisin, *amigão, onde tens estado?*" I stared at Oisin, hoping for a translation even though I kind of got the gist of it. He was no help. "Tu és mau. Já não me visitas há mais de um mês."

"What?" I couldn't help it. I got a word here and there but she was speaking too fast.

Oisin threw me a glance and laughed. "Better speak in English, Ana," he told the woman, who had stood up and thrown herself into the god's arms in an enthusiastic hug. I wasn't sure Taz would approve. "My friend doesn't speak much Portuguese."

Ana turned her face to me, her shortish, dark brown hair framing her pixie face in a profusion of curls. "Sorry, didn't realize," she said in perfect English.

"I was just telling Oisin I've missed him. He hasn't come to see me in a while."

Relieved she spoke English so well, I took a deep breath before speaking again. "Hi, my name is Aiden Mercer. I was wondering whether Luis Andrade is available." I assumed he was her boss or at least her supervisor since she sat outside his office. Mr. Andrade was obviously not the humble kind, for he had a giant sign over the office door with his name and the title *Director de Operações* in shiny golden letters. "We need to talk to him."

"He went out for cigarettes," Ana said with a disapproving frown, "but he shouldn't take long." She hesitated for a moment, took a look at Oisin, and smiled. "Why don't you guys wait in his office? I will bring you some coffee in a second. Sugar?"

While the young woman busied herself with the espresso machine set up on a small table across from her desk, we walked into Andrade's office and closed the door behind us. I wanted to have a good look before Ana came back.

My back was still turned when I heard the Irish god take a sharp intake of air.

"What happened?" I asked, spinning on my heels.

He didn't have to answer me. If we were still wondering whether Andrade had anything to do with the theft, this most definitely dissolved any lingering doubts. Draped over the small couch, against one of the walls of the small office, was a beautiful, blue merman tail.

* * *

"What do you mean he's not coming?" We waited in that office for so long we began wondering whether Andrade had gone to buy cigarettes in Spain. "I thought he just went out for a bit."

To her credit, the young receptionist looked contrite enough that I felt bad for my tone of voice. "That's what he said, but when he called a bit ago and I told him you were waiting to see him, he told me he wasn't coming back to the office today."

Weasel! He must have guessed what we were there for. "What about an address, Ana?" Oisin said softly, laying a hand on her shoulder and smiling. The young god had skills. "Maybe we can just go see him there. This is a matter of great importance."

Ana smiled back at him, her confidence restored. "Yes, I can do that," she said, beaming. "I will text it to you right now."

Oisin and I exchanged a meaningful look. Maybe not all was lost. We knew now he was the thief, so we could just give the address to Silva and let the police take care of the rest.

The receptionist retrieved her cell from her desk and punched in a few times. As soon as she stopped, Oisin's phone pinged. "Got it," he said, glancing at the screen. "Thank you, lovely."

While Ana and the Irish god flirted, my mind was working out scenarios of how to leave that place with the huge mertail without calling anyone's attention. It wasn't as if you could stuff it into a plastic bag. It was made of silicone, heavy, with large fins and bright blue scales. Would I be able to teleport with it? I had done it with Naël a few times, so it should work.

I poked Oisin's shoulder. "We probably should leave, my red-haired Irish friend. There is something *I* have to do." I emphasized the "I," hoping he would get my drift.

He did. "Well, Ana, call me when you have a chance, okay?" he said in a honeyed voice. "Até á vista, linda." Did every foreign in Portugal know how to speak Portuguese except me?

We hurried out of the building and as soon as we were around the bend, I thought myself into the office, hoping the receptionist had returned to her desk. Thankfully she had, and I was able to quietly grab hold of the tail and wish myself out of the studio and into

Oisin's car. Of course, I miscalculated where exactly in the car to wish myself into and ended up squished into the trunk. I left the tail there and teleported into the passenger seat to wait for my godly driver.

My life was very strange indeed. Others get driven around in Ubers. I have a god for a driver. But who's complaining?

CHAPTER 9

The Night Before the Wedding

Weddings were hard work. I'd never understand how brides put themselves —voluntarily—through the agony of a big wedding. I'd sooner elope than go through the mess of choosing a wedding gown and matching maid-of-honor dresses, the right flowers to decorate the wedding venue, the banquet afterward…. The mere thought of it made me cringe. Thankfully, Naël and I were on the same wavelength about our own ceremony; now that we had decided to get married on our subterranean beach, we planned for a very simple wedding surrounded by our small—but ever-growing —circle of friends.

"And unicorns," the fiendish tweener declared. I gave her the look of death, but it didn't faze her.

"Come on, Aiden, just a touch of unicorn, please. It's the most magical creature in the world, as unique as you and my brother."

Vee was evil with her sweet talk. "Unicorns don't exist." Or did they? I certainly had never seen one. "And both me and your brother do. So there!" Yep, still immature. Vee brought out that side of me more often than not. "No unicorns, little mermaid."

"Who says unicorns don't exist?" my husband-to-be interjected without bothering to look up from whatever he was reading on the kitchen island.

My jaw dropped. "Are you telling me they're real?" Not that I hadn't seen weirder things, but unicorns? "How come I have never seen one?"

Fouchard raised his gaze, one corner of his lips curled upward. "They are rare even among us magicals, but as real as you and me." He was pulling my leg, I was sure. Or was he? With my merrow it was hard to tell. "Vee, stop pestering my fiancé about it. You're going to make him rethink his decision to marry me."

I dropped the large sparkly star I was holding and sprung to my feet—I swear I heard a boing—to run and hug my merman. "I would never do that," I said, holding him tightly. "Even if you littered the place with unicorns."

He laughed and I heard Vee snort. "Good to

know," he said, his warm breath tickling my ear. "But rest assured I will not fill the place with the one-horned creature. Now can you let me go? You're squishing me."

I did as he asked but not before dropping a kiss on his delicious lips.

The stolen mertail had been safely delivered to Silva and I could finally focus solely on my wedding. Hard to do, though, in a house that was beginning to look like one of those Christmas wonderlands.

"Don't you think we have enough Christmas decorations, Vee?" There were so many fairy lights, tinsel, and festive unicorns on every wall, banister, door, and piece of furniture that I walked around with a semi-permanent glare in my eyes.

"You can never have enough decorations, Aiden," Vee said in a voice belonging to a wise old woman. That girl cracked me up. "Will you stop bellyaching and hang that star over the door? We still have to hang the mistletoe in the hallway."

That caught my attention. "I want mistletoe hung over every door in this house," I said, wistful and dreamy-eyed.

Fouchard chuckled, and Vee gave me the stink eye. "That's not the tradition, Aiden," said the twelve-year-old sage. "One is all."

I glared at her, tempted to stick my tongue out, and then looked pleadingly at my mate. "How would it hurt to have a few around the house?"

"It's not like you need an excuse to lip-lock your man." Freaking witch, always popping out of nowhere. "You don't need the mistletoe."

"Have you ever heard of knocking when visiting other people's houses?" I knew what the answer was but thought I'd ask anyway. "What if we were—" My eyes roamed to the little mermaid who looked at me expectantly. Dang! It was hard to have children in the house. "Well, you know, otherwise busy."

Taz laughed and took a seat at the high stools by the island. "Oh Aiden, ever so entertaining." She removed her trademark giant hat and set it down on the counter. "I came to take you away."

My head snapped up. "Take me away? What are you talking about, witch?"

"It's bad luck for the grooms to see each other the night before the wedding," she said, rummaging through the fruit bowl. "So, I'm taking you away to a hotel."

I squinted, the strong, acrid smell of a dead rat tickling my nose. "There is no such superstition," I protested, noticing my man suddenly becoming very interested in the view from the window. The rotten smell was getting stronger. "What are you plotting now?"

Taz raised her eyes from the fruit and pointed a long, red fingernail at me. "You never learn, do you? So suspicious of everyone, even your friends." In my defense, I had to be, considering the friends I had. "We are throwing you a little bachelor party at the hotel."

My mate was definitely avoiding my eyes. "Who is *we*? And what about Naël? Doesn't he get a bachelor party too?"

"Of course he does," the witch said, sliding onto her high heels. "Cristina and Silva are coming over in a bit and taking Fouchard out. You hit the jackpot and have me and Oisin as party sidekicks."

It wasn't that I didn't trust her—no, wait. That was exactly what it was. I trusted Taz in a life-and-death situation, but for mundane things like that, she was as trustworthy as an elf. Whatever they were hatching, my sexy merman was in on it too. Trusting Taz was iffy, but if my man was involved, I had to trust it was nothing bad.

I let out a loud exhale. "All right, I'll go with you," I said. "But you're not planning on anything that involves me getting killed, right?"

Taz walked around me and flattened her palms on my shoulder blades. "Go get what you need. We'll bring you back tomorrow afternoon right before the wedding." I threw another glance at Naël, who smiled in response. "Come on, Aiden, stop being difficult."

"Yes, Aiden, don't ruin the surprise." Just as she said it, Vee covered her own mouth with her hands. She had just spilled part of the beans. "I mean, the surprise Taz and Oisin have for you." *Too late, sweet mermaid. Way too late.* Taz opened her eyes so wide, I thought they might pop out of the sockets. If at first a little flustered, Vee recovered quickly, skipping up to me and lacing an arm through mine. "Don't be a party-pooper, Aiden."

Fouchard, who had been silent through most of the conversation, now joined in. "Sweetheart, why don't you let people do something nice for you." His smile melted the last thread of doubt I had. "Go and have fun. I will see you tomorrow for our wedding."

"Okay, okay," I growled, letting Taz and Vee push me out of the kitchen. "But when I come back, you better have mistletoe hanging from every door in this house."

"No need, Aiden," Fouchard yelled after us. "I will always kiss you any time you want me to."

I was almost by the door when I thought about one very important detail. I turned around for a moment and said, "And absolutely no unicorns at our wedding."

Vee pursed her lips and stomped on my foot. I yelped and Taz laughed. "Serves you right, druid-god," she said, right before Vee slammed the door on my face.

CHAPTER 10

Tails & Mistletoe...
Um, and Unicorns?

Cristina scanned me from head to toes, biting down on her lower lip, a hand cupping her chin in a poor imitation of Rodin's *The Thinker*. I was sweating and shaking. Nervous didn't even begin to describe how I felt as I went through wedding inspection—at least that's what I had decided to call Cristina's pre-ceremony assessment.

"Well? Do I pass muster?" I asked, wobbling on my jittery feet. "Do I look decent enough to be a husband?"

Cristina raised her eyes to mine, a solemn expression on her face, and placed her hands on her hips. "I don't know, Aiden," she started, shaking her head. "There is something off."

Panic closed my throat and sent my heart stampeding. "What? What's off?" I asked, looking down at my clothes and touching my pants, searching for some flaw somewhere. My groom and I didn't stand on formality, so my outfit was not your usual wedding threads. I had decided to go as myself, just a little dressier. Instead of my trademark shorts—which I wore even in the winter—I picked a pair of cropped gray chinos and a simple blue button-down linen shirt.

Cristina studied me for a little while longer as anxiety inflated in my chest, a balloon ready to explode. "I know what it is," she said suddenly. Taking a step forward, she aimed at my throat and grabbed the collar of my shirt, unbuttoning a couple of the top buttons. Then she took a step backward and admired her work. "Now it's perfect."

I let out a long exhale. "Do I really look good?"

The seriousness of her beautiful, scarred face melted away and was replaced by a sunny smile. "You look so handsome. Naël is going to love it." With a little hop, she threw herself in my arms and hugged me tightly. "My best friend looks so grown up." We both laughed, hanging on to each other. "I can't believe the man whore is getting married before I do."

We pulled away from each other, and Cristina smoothed out the wrinkles in my clothes with her hand. "But you're the first one to spawn," I quipped, pulling on the sides of my shirt.

She glanced up at me and chuckled. "Thank God. I'd be freaking out if you were pregnant," she said, her eyebrows arched high. "I'm still getting used to the idea you are some kind of god. Please don't throw another surprise into the equation."

On impulse, I leaned forward and planted a kiss on her forehead. "Thank you, Cristina," I whispered. She looked up at me, a question in her eyes. "For being my best friend. Until you came into my life, I didn't think it was possible anyone would care for me."

She blinked away what looked suspiciously like tears. "Fool. You may be an idiot but you're a lovable one." She rose on her tiptoes and kissed my cheek. "Now, I better take you to your *noivo* downstairs or the merman may die of anxiety."

We looped our arms together and walked down to the main floor where Silva was waiting. He looked absolutely stunning in a black tuxedo, his short black hair blending perfectly with the rest of the outfit. The warlock had style.

"It's about time," he said as soon as he saw us. "I thought I may have to call my men and launch a search party again."

Cristina gave me a tug. "It was my fault," she said

with a giggle that sounded more like a sob. "I wanted to be alone with my bachelor friend a little longer." She looked up at me and smiled. "Let's go get your merman."

I couldn't deny it; my legs were shaking as we made our way down the stairs to the basement, grateful for Cristina's support. The warlock cop followed us like a shadow, ready to step in if necessary. His protective hackles were always on red alert when it came to his fiancée. I held a whole lot of admiration and respect for him, however begrudgingly.

The humming of voices from the beach faded away as soon as we stepped on the sand. Good thing Cristina was still holding on to me because I would have fallen on my ass. My friends and husband-to-be had been busy. Thousands of fairy lights had been strung along the rock walls of the beach, bathing everything in an otherworldly glow. As I had requested, there were no frilly bows or flowery swags anywhere in sight, with the exception of the two large pots with floating white and pink lotus blooms flanking the spot where my beautiful merrow was. To my surprise, there was a small crowd in attendance: my mother, holding my father's hand, all the Capuchos monks in their nondescript brown habits, Taz with a spiffied up Oisin by her side, and even the little Einstein Oracle who had not bothered to change clothes and was unceremoniously sitting cross-legged on the sand.

My family.

My eyes burned with tears of joy. Vee, her wild, white curls bouncing around her cute, freckled face, skipped her way to us, holding a bouquet of water lilies. "The blushing groom is here," she shouted. I chuckled, a few sobs mixed in for good measure. Where in heaven's name had she learned that saying? She stopped short of slamming into me, leaned over, and whispered, "I'm your flower girl, by the way. And ring bearer. The rings are hiding in this bouquet." She pointed a skinny brown finger at the bow holding the lilies together. "You're not going to faint, are you? You look a bit pasty."

I was feeling a little woozy and congratulated myself for the decision not to wear any shoes. My toes sank into the cold sand and the energy from the earth flowed up my legs and into every nook and cranny of my nervous body.

"I'll be okay," I promised her in a semi-whisper. "Just stay close in case I need someone to slap me." Which she would gladly do. Her impish smile warmed my insides.

With the little mermaid behind us, we walked toward my mate, a vision in blue and white. He had been secretive about his choice of clothes. "Better to surprise you, my love," he'd said. My mouth watered as I ran my eyes over my mate's beautiful body. The royal blue button-down shirt he was wearing contrasted with the pure white of his trousers, his strong legs pushing against the fabric. He had rolled the sleeves up to his elbows, emphasizing his muscles.

For a moment we were all alone on that beach, his powerful arms holding me tight to never, ever let go.

"Don't want to spoil the fantasizing, but the wedding has to happen before you guys can get your freak on." Cristina's familiar voice snapped me out of my daydreaming, and I picked up the pace, suddenly anxious to be beside my man.

I stumbled on my own feet as I finally arrived between the two giant lotus-filled pots where my merman patiently awaited. He thrust out his hand to prevent me from falling and our eyes met. If there was anything inside of me that was not yet melted, I was now a vessel of nothing but gooey liquid. His fingers squeezed mine and I smiled what I was pretty sure was the goofiest smile ever. I was so besotted by this man. How was that even possible? How had I gone from a total man whore to a fiercely one-man guy?

"Are you ready to be my husband?" Naël whispered, a tiny grin on his lips.

Was I ever!

* * *

I wish I could say I remember every second of the ceremony, but I don't. Whatever words the minister—who turned out to be one of Neptune's minions—said before the final vows were lost in the maze of my attention span, focused as I was solely on my merman.

"Aiden, your vows." Cristina prodded me from behind with a very pointy nail. I came down from whatever cloud I had been flying on and tried to concentrate on what I had rehearsed so many times.

It took me a few tries to bring those lines from the recesses of my memory. Naël gave me an encouraging nod; I cleared my throat and started, "Naël Fouchard, you have to be the crankiest merman in the seven seas." He grinned and a few chuckles rippled through the small crowd in attendance. "We've been through a lot in such a short time, and I'll be honest; the old me would have hightailed out of this really fast." I reached out for his hand. "But I'm so glad I didn't, sweetheart. Meeting you has been the best thing that ever happened to me. Thanks to you, I learned how to love." I squeezed his hand, tears stubbornly burning in my eyes. "Thanks to you, I learned to be less biased and to accept who I am." I paused, fighting the tears semi-successfully. "But most of all, Naël, you gave me the family I always wanted and showed me what being loved feels like. I love you, now and forever."

There was applause from the crowd, and for a second, I felt bad for my parents. That speech was sincere, but it was certainly also hard for them to hear. They had left me as a baby to struggle through life in a world that was anything but kind toward a child who was gay and could see monsters no one else saw. I knew they loved me and I knew they'd be there for me from now on, but the past couldn't be changed, could it?

It was Fouchard's turn. He pulled me a bit closer as if afraid I wouldn't be able to hear him. "Aiden Mercer, you're the worst entrepreneur in the world but the luckiest demigod ever!" I snorted and he pulled me even closer. "You're lucky we met. You're lucky you're gorgeous and skilled in bed. You're lucky the earth itself loves you." All true. "But you know what? I'm even luckier to have sought your detective services when I was a murder suspect. Even more fortunate that you saw beyond my crankiness and rudeness to settle yourself firmly in my heart. I'm the luckiest merman in the world to have you in my life. I will most definitely love you forever." I discreetly wiped a tear off my cheek.

"Aiden Mercer and Naël Fouchard, will you take each other as your lawful wedded husband, for better and worse, in sickness and in health, on land and in water, forever united as one heart, one soul?" the handsome merman minister intoned in a singsong voice.

We both said our I-dos and Vee stepped forward with the rings. I slid the plain gold ring on his brown finger, my eyes never leaving his, and then it was his turn to do it.

"You are now married," the man said. "You may kiss your husband."

As more applause exploded around us, my new husband pointed up above us, where a small bunch of mistletoe hung suspended in the air. "I thought you might like it," he said with that naughty smile of his. "I also had Vee hang it all over the house just in case we need a reminder to kiss often and wholeheartedly."

We didn't.

Our lips met in our first married kiss, and it was total bliss. I didn't know how long we explored each other's mouths, tongues dancing together, our tastes mixing and mingling. We were married.

Fouchard pulled away first, lips swollen by love. "Before anything else, my love, I have a gift for you." He waved at someone in the back. "You have always said that you're sorry you can't swim like me, that there is a part of my life that will never be yours." I opened my mouth to protest but he raised a hand to stop me. "So, I bought you this." He pointed at someone who turned out to be the warlock.

We all looked at Silva as he dragged something big and heavy across the sand, heading toward us. As he got closer, I had the feeling I had seen it before, blue and glossy like my husband's tail.

"Wait! Is that the tail I recovered from the napper?" I yelled.

My merman chuckled. "Yes, except there was no tailnapping," he said, draping an arm over my shoulders. "It was all a ruse to keep you busy while we planned the wedding." My mouth opened and closed like an oyster in need of food. "I commissioned this tail from a very talented young silicone artist, Merman Icarus in California, so you could go along with me on my longer swims."

I had been struck speechless. I stared at the beautiful mertail in awe. Now that it was mine, I realized how much like Naël's it was. I ran a hand over it and smiled. "It's beautiful, Naël." His eyes met mine. "But I didn't get you a gift."

Before he could say anything, the whole beach echoed with the sound of *The Little Mermaid's* "Part of Your World" and everyone exploded into song. I laughed and hugged my new husband, delirious with happiness. Perfect wedding song for me.

Naël leaned over and whispered in my ear. "You can give me a present later on. After the reception, we're going to our love cave. You can be as generous as you want once we get there."

I burst out laughing, parts of me already getting a bit too excited. "Sweetheart, I'm going to make you the happiest groom ever."

We winked at each other and joined in the singing. I watched my family and friends, even Neptune, as they belted out the high notes of the song, voices mixed with laughter. Cristina and Silva holding on to each other. Taz and Oisin dancing in the sand. My mother and father, still holding hands. Vee... wait! Where was the little mermaid?

"Where's Vee?" I asked, raising my voice above the singing.

Naël pointed at the far end of the beach where the rock ceiling was higher. I couldn't believe my eyes; my new sister-in-law was riding a white steed. Not just a regular horse, but a sparkling white one, with a beautiful flowing mane and a horn.

"How?" Unicorns were real? Where had this one come from? I had so many questions.

My husband just laughed, tucked me in under his

arm, and kissed my forehead. "This is the world you just married into, sweetheart. One surprise after another," he said.

A few months ago, I would have probably freaked out a bit, but now the magical world didn't scare or worry me anymore.

All was perfect now that I was part of Naël's world.

Thank you for reading, *Of Tails & Mistletoe*, the conclusion of the Of Magic & Scales series. If you enjoyed this series, then maybe you'll also enjoy my other M/M paranormal romances, **_Infinite Blue_** and **_Lavender Fields_**.

I also have a fabulous epic M/M fantasy to check out too, **Sleeping Love.**

Acknowledgments

It may sound strange, but I want to thank my cast of characters for gifting me with some of the best writing moments of my life. I feel I created friends instead of fictional characters. They kept me company throughout a crazy pandemic year, they made me laugh and brought back memories of my country and my family. I wouldn't be surprised if I revisit these guys in the future.

Many thanks go to my publisher for the faith she has placed in my stories. I'll never be able to thank you enough, Becky.

A million and one (because a million isn't nearly enough) thanks to the Hot Tree staff (editors, formatters, graphic designers, marketers, everyone) who are amazing not only at what they do but for all the support they are always willing to give me.

To my awesome PA, Barb, who can post a thousand promos in under a minute (no kidding, she's a wizard). Your help and support are priceless.

A heartfelt thanks to Merman Icarus, whose work

inspired the subplot in this book. Go check out his Instagram page. The man is a master at creating merfolk accessories for all the real-life merpeople out there.

Family and friends in Portugal, I love you and miss you. Family and friends in the US, I love you and thank you for your support.

Readers, you're the best. I will never be able to thank you all enough for your support. Keep reading and keep being merfolk even if only in your imagination and within the pages of a book.

Thanks for reading *Of Tails and Mistletoe*. I do hope you enjoyed this story. I appreciate your help in spreading the word, including telling a friend. Before you go, it would mean so much to me if you would take a few minutes to write a review and share how you feel about my story so others may find my work. Reviews really do help readers find books. Please leave a review on your favorite book site.

Don't miss out on New Releases, Exclusive Giveaways and much more!

Join my newsletter: http://bit.ly/reisnewsletter
Join my reader group: http://bit.ly/RebelsOutcasts

I'd love to hear from you directly, too. Please feel free to e-mail me at

catarinadeobidos1@gmail.com or check out my website http://bit.ly/WebNatalina for updates.

Natalina wrote her first romance in collaboration with her best friend at the age of 13. Since then she has ventured into other genres, but romance is first and foremost in almost everything she writes.

After earning a degree in tourism and foreign languages, she worked as a tourist guide in her native Portugal for a short time before moving to the United States. She lived in three continents and a few islands, and her knack for languages and linguistics led her to a master's degree in education. She lives in Virginia where she has taught English as a Second Language to elementary school children for more years than she cares to admit.

Natalina doesn't believe you can have too many books or too much coffee. Art and dance make her happy and she is pretty sure she could survive on lobster and bananas alone. When she is not writing or stressing over lesson plans, she shares her life with her husband and two adult sons.

facebook.com/authornatalinareis

twitter.com/TichaB

instagram.com/reisnatalina

bookbub.com/authors/natalina-reis

About the Publisher

Hot Tree Publishing opened its doors in 2015 with an aspiration to bring quality fiction to the world of readers. With the initial focus on romance and a wide spread of romance subgenres, Hot Tree Publishing has since opened their first imprint, Tangled Tree Publishing, specializing in crime, mystery, suspense, and thriller.

Firmly seated in the industry as a leading editing provider to independent authors and small publishing houses, Hot Tree Publishing is the sister company to Hot Tree Editing, founded in 2012. Having established in-house editing and promotions, plus having a well-respected market presence, Hot Tree Publishing endeavors to be a leader in bringing quality stories to the world of readers.

Interested in discovering more amazing reads brought to you by Hot Tree Publishing? Head over to the website for information:

www.hottreepublishing.com

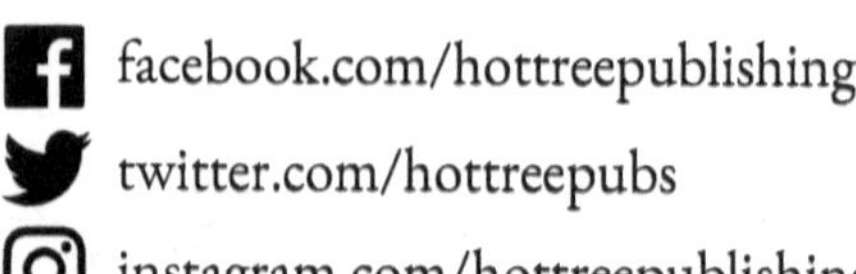

facebook.com/hottreepublishing
twitter.com/hottreepubs
instagram.com/hottreepublishing